SARAH M. ANDERSON

To my mom.
Here's to new beginnings and fresh starts!
Love you!

One

"It's a good crowd tonight," Kyle Morgan said as he slipped down the narrow hallway that qualified as the backstage of the Bluebird Cafe in Nashville, Tennessee. He winked at Brooke Bonner. "But I don't think any of them came for me."

Brooke gave the older man a shaky smile but didn't stop humming to herself. The Bluebird was usually full—it was a small space where songwriters and singers came to test out new material. She'd been coming here for a decade now—first as a patron, then as a performer. She hadn't been back in almost a year and a half, though.

She hadn't been anywhere since she'd had Bean.

This night marked the beginning of her official comeback. After almost seven months of what felt like house arrest, she was walking back into the spotlight.

She was done hiding.

Mostly done, anyway. No one but a few select people knew about James Frasier Bonner—who she still called Bean, even though he definitely had grown. At three months, Bean was already smiling and cooing at her.

He had his father's smile.

Kyle wasn't in the know about Bean. Which made Brooke feel bad because Kyle was almost a father figure to her. He'd been at the Bluebird for her very first show and had taught her more about songwriting than anyone else. At every step of Brooke's journey from "girl with a guitar" to "country music phenomenon," Kyle had been a cheerleader, giving her advice and gentle pushes forward.

"Missed seeing you around," Kyle said. "Been quiet without you."

If she could've picked a father, Kyle might've done the trick. Sadly, Crissy Bonner would never tell Brooke who'd sired her. And the fact that she was walking in her mother's footsteps by keeping Bean's father a secret was a huge problem for Brooke.

But what choice did she have?

She didn't *want* to repeat the mistakes her mother had made. She wanted to do better.

But first, she had to get back out into the music scene.

Kyle's smile crinkled the lines around his mouth. It was a damn shame he refused to even talk to Mom. They could've made a good couple, and Kyle was rocking a silver-fox thing. Plus, if Mom had had a boyfriend or a husband, it might've taken some of Crissy Bonner's focus off Brooke. But the few times Brooke had managed to get them in the same room, the barely concealed hatred had been enough to crush any dreams of an instant family.

Of course, if Kyle and Crissy had hooked up, that might've meant Brooke wouldn't have a Grammy and a couple of chart toppers to her name. And it also might've meant she'd never have performed at that All-Stars Rodeo where Flash Lawrence had been riding, which would've meant no Bean. And she loved her son with her whole heart.

"Does this show mean you're off hiatus?" Kyle asked as he packed up his guitar.

"Yup. I'd been touring for almost four years straight before I hit big last year. It just wiped me out."

That was the official position her record label and family had cooked up. Brooke had needed a break to work on her new material. There might have been something in there about resting her vocal cords, she couldn't remember.

It'd all been a load of crap.

No one *rested* during the last three months of pregnancy. New mothers with fussy babies didn't *rest*.

Not for the first time, Brooke wished they'd just announced she was pregnant and dealt with the issue head-on. Yeah, the press might've been brutal—but there was no such thing as bad PR, and she'd argued that her surprise pregnancy might've taken her second album, *White Trash Wonder*, from double to triple platinum. After all, an unexpected pregnancy was on brand.

She'd been overruled because of one fact and one fact alone: she wouldn't tell anyone who Bean's father was. Not that it was any of their business, because it wasn't.

Her mother hadn't forgiven her yet for sitting on that particular secret, as if Crissy hadn't done the exact same thing by refusing to acknowledge Brooke's father.

Which meant Brooke was stuck lying, which she hated.

Kyle stood and wrapped an arm awkwardly around her shoulder. "Welcome back," he said, giving her a friendly squeeze before he headed out to the front to watch. "You need anything, you just give me a call. I mean it, Brooke—anything at all."

Brooke's eyes stung with unexpected emotion at Kyle's thoughtfulness. She forced her shoulders down and started humming again, keeping her vocal cords warm.

Alex Andrews, her bodyguard and friend, squeezed her big frame into the hallway and handed Brooke a mug of hot tea. "They found some honey," she practically growled.

Brooke accepted the tea gratefully and took a sip. Ah, the perfect temperature. "Thanks, hon."

Alex was big and gruff, but underneath her tanklike exterior she was a softie with a heart of solid gold. They'd been friends since junior high, back when Brooke was a band geek just starting to perform and Alex had been the first girl to play offensive lineman on the football team. Long before *White Trash Wonder* had hit big, Alex had been right beside Brooke in every dive bar and county fair, doing her best to keep away grabby, drunk assholes.

Thirteen months ago, Alex had stayed home because her girlfriend had the flu, instead of joining Brooke in Fort Worth for the All-Around All-Stars Rodeo. If Alex had come, would Brooke and Flash have spent that white-hot night together? Or would Alex have been the voice of reason, keeping Brooke far away from cocky cowboys who were good in bed? And against the wall? And on the floor?

Brooke must have been frowning, because Alex asked, "Worried?"

Damn it—it was hard to get anything past that woman. Especially since Alex was one of the few people who knew about Bean. "It's fine. He's home with Mom," she said, stretching her facial muscles to loosen them up.

"They'll do great. Crissy only wants what's best for him," Alex replied, which was probably supposed to be reassuring. Except it wasn't and Alex knew it. Her eyes widened as she realized what she'd said. "Oh, crap—I didn't mean…"

"It's fine," Brooke repeated, taking this opportunity to test out her fake smile. Crissy Bonner's favorite saying was 'It's for the best.' Brooke starting singing lessons at the age of five was *for the best*. Guitar lessons at the age of six was *for the best*. Hours of practice every day were *for the best*. Slumber parties, birthday parties, pets or boys— they *weren't* for the best.

Just to be sure, she turned in her seat to wave at the people behind her who were still clapping.

Damn. There, at the bar—a long, lean cowboy was perched on the last seat, the brim of his black cowboy hat throwing his face into deep shadow. He wore jeans with an absolutely huge belt buckle, with a leather biker jacket over a black Western-style button-up shirt. She couldn't see his eyes, but she could feel him looking at her.

Oh, no. Oh, *hell*.

Maybe she was wrong. It wasn't like cowboys of a certain height and weight wearing black hats and big belt buckles didn't exist around Nashville because they absolutely did. But her blood pounded in her veins and her hands shook, and there was no mistaking the flight or fight reaction.

Because she wasn't wrong.

The cowboy shifted in his seat, tilting his head back. His gaze collided with Brooke's, and even though she hadn't seen him for thirteen months, even though she'd only ever spent one amazing night with him, heat pooled low in her belly and she trembled with want.

Her big mistake was sitting less than thirty feet away. The one time she'd gone off schedule and done something just for herself—not for her career or her mother or anyone—and she'd been paying the price ever since. She loved her son, but...

She wasn't ready. Not for Flash Lawrence.

Not for any of this.

The lights dimmed and an expectant hush fell over the crowd.

Well. The show had to go on, so Brooke did the only thing she could.

"It's so good to be back, y'all. I've been working on new material for my next album—should be out in a few months—and we're thinking of calling it *Your Roots Are*

Showing." The crowd laughed appreciatively as she flipped her hair back with an exaggerated toss of her head. "Aw, you guys are great."

She desperately wanted to turn in her seat for this next part. If that was Flash, what would he think when he heard the song title? But she didn't. She was giving him nothing to work with, and, besides, there was a literal audience here tonight. All it would take for the wildfire of gossip to catch and burn would be one too-long look, one touch, one wrong move, and her comeback would be forever tainted.

So she didn't turn, didn't even acknowledge that there was anyone behind her. She played to the people she could see when she said, "So the first song that'll be on the new album that I want to sing tonight is called 'One-Night Stand.'"

Two

God, she looked amazing.

Brooke Bonner wasn't wearing the skintight crop top and leather miniskirt she'd had on the last time Flash had seen her. For this small crowd, she was wearing a black hippy-style skirt that came just below her knees and showed off her turquoise cowboy boots. A long sweater vest thing without sleeves was held in place over a deep-cut white shirt with the kind of studded belt that Flash's sister Chloe sold for her Princess of the Rodeo clothing line.

Turquoise dripped off her ears and around her neck but—he had to lean to the side to see—her fingers were bare. He couldn't tell for sure, but he didn't think there was even a tan line for an engagement ring on her finger.

Thank God.

When she'd disappeared from the public eye a few months ago, Flash had been terrified to think she might have met someone, might have gotten married. If she had, he'd have had to walk out the Bluebird's door without a look back. He wasn't going to screw up a marriage. But no ring meant he settled in and ordered another ginger ale. He was here for the duration.

Had he ever seen a more beautiful woman? He'd met a lot of hot women and slept with his fair share of them, but there was something about the way Brooke was put together that drew his eye. He couldn't look away, hadn't been able to since the very first moment he'd seen her in Fort Worth. He'd kissed her hand and that had been that.

Brooke wasn't wearing a hat tonight, so he could see the glory of her dark red hair as it flowed down her back in long waves. His fingers itched to bury themselves in that hair, wrap it around his fist like he'd done the last time, holding her head so he could kiss her again and again.

Apparently, absence really did make the heart grow fonder, because Flash was so glad to see Brooke right now that he wanted to sweep her into his arms and carry her far, far away from this crowded little place and show her how damned glad he was to see her.

He'd spent a year trying not to miss this woman. A year of trying to put the most intense sexual experience of his life out of his mind. He'd tried to pick up buckle bunnies since that night, but he hadn't succeeded. Not once in thirteen months.

He was afraid Brooke Bonner had ruined him for any other woman.

And that would be a damn shame.

No way in hell he wanted to be tied down. Especially not this year, when the All-Around All-Stars Cowboy of the Year was in his sights. After a wreck of a year—mostly brought on by Flash's own hot temper and alcohol-fueled brawls—he was back and ready to prove he wasn't just a chip on his shoulder with a good right hook.

For too long, people had assumed that Flash only won the All-Stars because the Lawrence family owned the circuit, and he understood now that most of his fights had been about proving he wasn't just a Lawrence, but that when it came to the rodeo, he was one of the best.

Getting suspended from the rodeo after that last fight—along with forfeiting his winnings up to that point—had been a blessing, although it sure hadn't felt like it at the time, especially not with the busted jaw Flash had gotten brawling. But it'd forced him to come to grips with his temper and grow the hell up. Plus, it'd shown everyone the All-Stars wasn't just a family business coddling the baby of the family. The rodeo family understood now that Flash had earned his place in the rankings.

This was *his* year and, for once, he wasn't going to shoot himself in his own foot. That included this thing between him and Brooke.

He just wanted…well, he wanted another night with her, to see if there was still that same electric current between them.

Best case, they'd make an effort to meet up on the road a few times a year, whenever his rodeo was in town during her concerts. He wouldn't say no to something like that. Not with her. He could focus on winning it all and she could focus on her career, and they'd get the chance to enjoy themselves during their downtime, like they had in Texas.

Then she announced the name of her first new song. "One-Night Stand."

The tips of Flash's ears went hot. That wasn't about him, right?

Couldn't be. It was the height of egotism to think that one night with him had left Brooke with anything other than a fond memory.

"Everyone should have one good night stand, don't you think?" Brooke went on, and the crowd chuckled approvingly. Someone to his left wolf whistled. Flash didn't see who, but he'd like to bust whoever it was in the jaw.

But the moment that thought crossed his mind, Flash clamped down on it. He was not going to lose his temper here. People were allowed to be jerks. He wasn't responsible for teaching them the errors of their ways when they crossed the line. Throwing a punch to defend Brooke's honor was something the old Flash would've done. The new-and-hopefully-improved Flash settled for glaring in the direction of the whistler.

Besides, causing a scene didn't serve his goals. He wanted to get reacquainted with Brooke Bonner. He needed to find out if there was something worth chasing between them or if he just needed to man up and move on.

If he got lucky, then he'd get lucky. If not, well, he still had to win it all.

The All-Around All-Stars Rodeo was in Nashville this weekend and he'd been hoping to find a way to run into her. When she'd posted on social media she'd be at the Bluebird tonight, he'd driven like a bat out of hell to get to Tennessee five days early just to see her.

At the bare minimum, he needed to make things right between them. Starting a brawl less than two minutes into her set would pretty much guarantee he'd never get another shot. So he kept a lid on his temper and took another drink of his soda.

When the crowd settled down, Brooke leaned in close to the microphone and said, "I'm so glad to see so many people agree—it's my favorite piece of furniture, too!"

Flash let out a slow breath, grinning in spite of his nerves. He'd loved her snarky sense of humor last year, too. She hadn't fawned over him and he had done his best not to fawn over her. There'd been an…understanding between them, almost. And a woman with a sense of humor was surprisingly erotic.

Thank goodness that a year of superstardom hadn't changed that about her.

Then Brooke began to sing as she played her guitar, and something in Flash's chest let go as the sound of her voice washed over him. By God, he'd missed the hell out of her.

She might not remember him—although, given how her eyes had widened slightly when they'd made eye contact, he thought maybe she did. And she might not want to see him again. But for a little while, he could lose himself in her world.

Until he realized what she was singing.

"It's just a one-night stand,
No tomorrow, no plans."

Well, damn. Yeah, she remembered him. But it wasn't a good thing. Especially not when she got to the chorus.

"You weren't worth the fun.
My one-night stand."

And the hell of it was, it was a great song. She had the audience eating out of the palm of her hand.

"Don't want to hear your excuses,
I don't care about your plans.
Not waiting any longer.
Screw your demands.
It's time I made my one-night stand."

Chills raced down his back as she held the last note, strong and powerful. He hadn't even had the chance to say hello and she was already shutting him down.

When the song ended, she did not look at him. She didn't sneak a peek out of the corner of her eye, didn't pivot in her chair, nothing. If she'd recognized him, it was clear she was ignoring him. "Whoo, y'all like that? That's just the beginning—I have a whole album of sass coming your way!"

Anger—an old, familiar feeling—began to push through his veins, but Flash refused to let it win. It was entirely possible that Brooke Bonner had forgotten all about him after her whirlwind breakout year. There was also a distinct possibility that, if she did remember him, she didn't hold him in any particularly high esteem.

He should've anticipated the song, though. He should've anticipated her anger. Anger was his second language. It came as naturally to him as breathing. But he hadn't seen this *attack* coming.

Okay, yeah, there'd been a superhot one-night stand. They'd hooked up in her dressing room before the show, which had made her late to go on because leather miniskirts weren't easy to work around. And it'd been good.

God, he still went hard just thinking about taking her against the wall in that tiny room, staring into her eyes as they both fought not to make a single sound. So damn *good*. And she had to have agreed, right? Because he'd hung around after the show, and when she'd seen him waiting for her, her entire face had lit up and she'd crooked her finger at him. They'd spent the rest of the night wrapped around each other in her hotel suite, having hot sex and ordering room service and, in between the seductions, making each other laugh.

They'd parted friends the next morning. He'd made damn sure to leave her with a smile on her face. He knew he hadn't stopped grinning for days. Weeks, even.

So how had they gotten from *that* to *this*?

"My next song—now just wait for it," she all but purred into the mike, "is called 'How Many Licks' because that was always the question, right?" The crowd hooted. "How many licks to get to the center of the sucker?"

"Three!" some jackass yelled.

"As many licks as it takes," a different ass yelled. Brooke wagged a scolding finger at him.

Flash had to close his eyes and focus on his breathing. Behind his eyelids, the world was red. They weren't disrespecting her. She'd chosen that title to get that exact reaction. She knew what she was doing and it wasn't his job to defend her from every slight. He'd already tried that once and had the criminal record—and nemesis—to prove it. He'd busted Tex McGraw up pretty damn good because the man had dared to put Brooke's name in his mouth.

Obviously, Flash understood why Tex hated him with a white-hot fury—Flash had knocked the man out of the All-Stars with a solid right hook. But Tex hadn't let up any with his online attacks since then, and he sure as hell hadn't accepted either of Flash's apologies—not the court-mandated one and not the more sincere one Flash had made after a few months of sobriety. But it was fine. Flash had gotten to a place in his life where he could handle online swipes from Tex without being driven to fits of rage. That was how far Flash had come in a year.

Brooke launched into the song, which cut off any other outbursts. The red haze behind his eyes faded, and he was able to breathe without feeling like punching someone.

Not surprisingly, this song felt personal, too. The double entendres flew fast and furious, but the core of the song was about a guy who couldn't take his licks and bailed.

A lot of people didn't like Flash. He'd never made it particularly easy for anyone to like him, but at least he knew it. However, he'd never inspired such strong feelings that someone could write an entire album based on how much they hated him, for God's sake.

Right. Instead of being insulted and letting it get to him, he was going to focus on feeling…flattered. Yeah, flattered. Not just any rodeo rider had an entire album dedicated to him, officially or unofficially. And if she publicly acknowledged that he was the inspiration, well, Flash was sure that his sister, Chloe, would find a way to spin Brooke's new album as a positive for Flash and the All-Around All-Stars Rodeo. Probably.

Besides, Brooke had said herself the album wouldn't be out for a few more months. She was still fine-tuning some of the material, still recording. Forewarned was forearmed. It was a good thing he was here tonight. He could work with Chloe to plan for a couple of different contingencies.

His sister had already basically figured out that Flash was crushing hard on Brooke.

Although...she'd want to know why Brooke was so furious with him. And he did not have an answer for that. Brooke had kissed him goodbye. Thanked him for the amazing night. Told him to take care.

And that was *it*.

At least she hadn't forgotten him, right? If there was one word that described Flash Lawrence, it was *memorable*.

When Brooke started the next song—titled "Not Going Down (Without a Fight)"—Flash almost couldn't take it. What the hell? If it'd been any other club or dive bar in Nashville, he would've bailed. But when a songwriter or a singer started their set at the Bluebird, no one moved and no one talked—house rules. So he had no choice but to sit there and listen.

He'd spent a year trying to make sense of the fact that Brooke Bonner was an itch he hadn't finished scratching. Before her, he'd bounced around bars and rodeos for four, maybe five years, picking up buckle bunnies and beautiful women in every town from Phoenix to Peoria while riding on the All-Stars circuit. Brooke Bonner should've been just one more woman. It'd been a one-night. Meaningless. Satisfying.

Except that that night had meant something to him and he'd spent nearly thirteen months unsatisfied.

Coming here tonight hadn't been a good idea. But damn it, he needed to know if their night together had meant anything to her.

Something more than raw material.

Finally, her set ended and the crowd came back to life. Because she was the last act, she stayed in the center of the room and signed autographs and posed for pictures. Flash hung back at the bar, debating his next move. Should he wait for the crowd to thin and then approach her? Or would it be better if they didn't have an audience? In that case, he should head out to the parking lot and wait by her car. Or was that too creepy?

Brooke glanced at him, a frown wrinkling her forehead before she quickly looked away. Nothing about that said *invitation*.

But he didn't care about that little frown. He didn't care about the songs or the radio silence that had lasted over a year.

He wanted to look her in the eye, make his case and then hear whatever she needed to get off her chest in person—without losing his temper. He wanted to know how they'd gotten from that wild night to this.

And if he didn't get lucky…he'd walk.

But he wasn't playing this guessing game.

He paid his tab and headed outside. The Bluebird was in a nondescript strip mall, and it took some work for Flash to work his way around to the back of the building. There—that plain sand-colored sedan had to be hers. She'd told him that she drove a boring car because it blended in.

He took up residence against a wall a good ten feet from the door of the Bluebird, giving her plenty of room. Lying in wait for her was a terrible idea, especially after that window into her mind and most especially after that frown. Frankly, he wouldn't be surprised if she pulled a gun on him.

But that was a risk he was willing to take.

Three

"Great set," Kyle said, a note of pride in his voice. "It's going to be a massive hit. The whole album. Very girl power. I wish I'd written half of it."

"Be sure to tell the record label that, okay?" Brooke said, her cheeks beginning to hurt with all the smiling she was doing. She valued Kyle's opinion and the crowd had seemed to enjoy the songs as well, so this was all great.

Except Flash Lawrence was here. What was she supposed to do now?

"I'm so proud of you," Kyle added, giving her an awkward hug.

She hugged him back but her mind was stuck on Flash. She'd almost, *almost* gone up to him out there. There were a lot of people milling around, so it wouldn't have been a big deal if she'd walked up to the bar and asked for something else to drink, right? People wouldn't have made any connection between her getting a drink and making small talk with a random cowboy, right? Then she could've at least figured out why he was here. The only two possibilities she could think of were—this was either a stunning coincidence or...

Or he'd come to see her.

And as she had only mentioned the Bluebird appearance on her Twitter feed two days ago…

She'd bet good money Flash was outside waiting for her. Which meant she had to talk to him. Which meant she had to tell him about Bean. Her son.

His son.

Oh *God*, this was going to suck.

"Hey," Kyle said, putting a hand on her arm. "You okay?"

"Fine," she said, working hard for that smile. She'd kept Bean a secret for a lot of good reasons, but none of them came to mind now that she knew she'd *have* to tell Flash. Because the alternative was to do exactly what her mother had done—keep on hiding and lying for the rest of her life—and Brooke couldn't do it. She was done hiding.

Or would be, just as soon as Flash knew. But to Kyle, she said, "Just relieved the new stuff is solid."

Kyle gave her a worried look. "You sure? I know you, Brooke. I know how you write. That stuff…it seemed kind of personal."

"We need to get going," Alex said, all but hip checking Kyle into a wall. Bless her heart. "Sorry, Morgan."

"Jeez, woman," Kyle said, rubbing his shoulder. "You should've stuck with football."

Brooke gave him another quick hug and made a not-exactly-quick stop in the ladies' room. Damn it, she was stalling.

Not hiding anymore, she repeated to herself as she picked up her guitar case. Alex opened the back door for her and, as she walked out into the humid Tennessee air, Brooke felt it again—that tingling at the base of her spine.

"Brooke."

That was all he had to say for her worst nightmares and her fondest dreams to come true at once because this was really happening.

Flash had come for her.

Oh, God—she wasn't going to be strong enough because even just the sound of her name on his lips was making her resolve weaken.

It didn't have the same effect on Alex. "Hey—back off," she rumbled, stepping in front of Brooke. "Show's over, buddy."

"Brooke?" Flash said again. "I just want to talk. Privately."

Yeah, she knew what happened when she and Flash had any privacy. At least the first time they'd hooked up, in her dressing room, she hadn't planned to have sex with him. At least, not right then. But Flash was that rare, dangerous creature—an irresistible man.

Okay, so not total privacy. But maybe semiprivate would work.

Brooke put a hand on Alex's shoulder. "It's okay," she said quietly as she stepped around her friend. "I know him."

Alex leaned down to whisper, "I don't like him." Of course, her whispering wasn't exactly quiet and, given Flash's smirk, it was clear he'd heard.

Yeah, neither would Crissy Bonner. The record label executives would love Flash, though—a showy pro-rodeo cowboy would be great for PR.

But she didn't want Flash to be a public relations bonanza. She wanted…hell. She didn't know what she wanted. Except for some privacy. She owed him that much.

"It's fine. Can you wait in the car?"

Alex glared at Flash and growled. But then she said, "Fine—but only for a few minutes," as she took the guitar case from Brooke.

Then he did the ballsy thing and approached Alex. "Hi. Flash Lawrence. And you are?"

Alex gave him a look that made lesser men turn tail and run, but Flash held his ground. He wasn't a coward, that much was for certain.

With a quick look at Brook, Alex said, "Alex Andrews.

Don't try anything funny." She jabbed a finger in Flash's direction and pointedly did *not* shake his hand.

"Wouldn't dream of it. As Brooke can tell you, I don't have a sense of humor." She couldn't help the smile that danced over her lips at that bold-faced lie. She remembered quite well how easily she'd laughed with Flash. It would've been one thing if he'd just been amazing between the sheets. But he'd been so dang easy to be with—kind and funny and tender and hot and...

He'd made her like him.

She'd liked him a good deal. Seeing all those news headlines about his violent temper and plea deals had felt like a betrayal, almost.

Because she'd been wrong about him.

Had any of it been real?

Flash stood his ground as Alex crowded into his personal space on her way to the car. The one with the baby bucket-seat base in the back seat. True, there was a blanket thrown over it because God forbid anyone should notice that Brooke Bonner had a child restraint system in her car, but still. Hard evidence of Bean was practically within line of sight.

How was she supposed to do this, damn it?

Because Flash looked so much better in person than he did in her dreams. Maybe it was just the jacket. But maybe it was him. There was something almost...calm about him.

With a huff, Alex slammed the driver's side door. It wasn't like Brooke and Flash were alone—the door to the Bluebird's kitchen was still propped open and Kyle might come out at any second. But for this brief moment, she and Flash had something resembling privacy.

"You look great," Flash began.

Brooke barely managed to avoid rolling her eyes even as the compliment sent a thrill through her. She was still at least one size above where she'd been before she'd gotten pregnant, and her mother was pushing her hard to lose the last of the baby weight so people wouldn't get suspicious. To know she looked okay was a relief.

No, no—she was not falling for superficial compliments. Because that was just the generic sort of statement that any man trying to get laid would open up with.

"What do you want, Flash?"

Please don't say something romantic ran through her mind in the key of G at the exact same moment *say something romantic* did the same thing in harmony. She'd have to write that down later—could be a good hook.

Flash whipped off his hat and launched the smile at her that had melted her heart—and other parts—so long ago. "I wanted to see you again, but I get the feeling that you're not exactly happy with me right now."

"You picked up on that, did you?"

"It was subtle," he replied, that easy grin on his lips, "but I did notice a little anger in those songs."

"Well, your powers of deduction are in fine form." She made a move to step around him, but he mirrored her movements. "What, Flash? I'm tired."

"I want to apologize," he said, moving closer.

She inhaled sharply. This sounded like a trap. "Oh? And what, exactly, are you apologizing for?"

"Don't know. But—" he went on when Brooke scoffed heartily "—clearly I hurt you and, judging by the songs I heard tonight—which were great—I hurt you badly. So let me apologize, Brooke."

Lord, did he have to sound so damned earnest about it? She almost wished he was cocky and overconfident. This would be so much easier if he was trying to talk his way into her panties again. This time, she'd be ready for him. This time, she wouldn't make a mistake.

But, no—the cocky cowboy she'd taken to bed was no-where to be seen, and in his place stood a serious man staring at her with so much longing and tenderness that, if Brooke allowed herself to think about it at all, he might take her breath away. So she didn't think about it.

"Fine. Apology accepted. Good night, Flash."

"Brooke," he said, her name a whisper on his lips. "I've missed you so much and the hell of it is, I don't know why."

"Really?" she snapped at him. *Anger* was great. *Anger* was not being seduced by his sweet words or intense looks. *Anger* was reminding her exactly who he was—a smooth talker with a violent streak—and, more importantly, who she was. He'd gotten her pregnant and she'd had to deal with the fallout without him because she couldn't trust him. Her whole life had been upended because of this man because she'd fallen for his sweet words and right now, he wasn't even that smooth at the talking. "That's not an apology, Flash. That's an insult."

"Would you listen?" he said, a warning in his voice. But then the weirdest thing happened—he took a step back and drew in a deep breath before letting it out slowly. "What I mean to say is, you were amazing—gorgeous and funny and smart and so easy to be with, and I'd be a fool not to want more of that. With you," he added quickly.

She snorted again, crossing her arms in front of her chest as different harmonies for *don't say something romantic* played in her mind.

"We had one night. A one-night stand, as you so eloquently put it." He ran a hand through his hair and then looked at her again, and this time the need in his eyes really did take her breath away. "That was all it was supposed to be, damn it, and…and it wasn't. Not for me. I wanted more with you then and I want more with you now."

"That's all well and good, Flash, but it's not enough. Not for me."

She needed to tell him about Bean. It wasn't fair to him

to keep his son hidden away, and it wasn't fair to Bean to deprive him of his father when the man was right here.

But she couldn't.

Not until she knew what he wanted and not if all he wanted was another night. Because she couldn't make a mistake like Flash Lawrence again. She needed him to be a father to his son. She needed him to be a co-parent, at the very least.

She needed to know she could trust him. And right now?

Not a lot of trust to go around.

Eyes closed, he took another one of those weirdly deep breaths and then he stepped up to her. Even though the night was warm and sticky, she felt the warmth from his body as if he'd shined the heat of the sun down upon her. And it only got worse when his hand came up to cup her face and his thumb stroked over her cheek. She knew she should push him away, but when he touched his forehead to hers she couldn't help leaning into his touch, breathing in the clean scent of him—leather and man and, Lord, it was wonderful.

"I followed your career, watched your climb up the charts. Celebrated your number-one hits and cheered your award-show wins. Saw your face every night I closed my eyes," he said, his voice soft as his breath brushed over her skin like a lover's kiss. Her body clenched in an involuntary response to his touch, his words. His *everything*. "I tried so hard to forget you, but I couldn't. And I'm so sorry."

He wasn't making any sense. He *wasn't*. But damn it all if he wasn't reminding her exactly why she'd taken him into her bed, because even when he was speaking in riddles he still made it sound so good—and feel even better. "Because you can't forget me?"

"No." He laughed a little. She looked deep into his eyes and saw unflinching honesty as he said, "I'll never be sorry for that. But I looked you up and I realized, what if you'd looked me up, too? What if you read about the arrest and trial and plea deals? So I'm sorry for how you must've felt when you read the headlines. I'm sorry you saw the worst of me, playing out in real time on the internet. I'm sorry I destroyed a perfect memory of a perfect night, because that's what you were to me. A perfect memory."

She inhaled sharply, her eyes stinging even as she squeezed them tight. That was a *very* good line, one that was already weaving its way into the chorus her brain was trying to write.

"I came here tonight not to tell you I wanted you—although I do," Flash went on. His other hand settled in the curve of her hip, gently pulling her into him and, weak as she was, she let him.

Her breasts brushed against his chest. "Then why?" she whispered, afraid of his answer even as she was desperate to hear it.

"I came here to tell you what happened after the headlines. After I got sentenced and suspended from the circuit, I did my community service and completed my anger management courses. I made a promise to myself and my family that I was going to rein in my anger and stop letting it rule me."

"You did?" Somehow, her hand was underneath his jacket on his chest—not pushing him away but resting right over his heart. She could feel it beating, strong and steady.

He turned his head ever so slightly, his lips brushing against her temple, then down her cheek. "I also quit drinking. I won't say I'm an alcoholic, but when I drank I couldn't keep a handle on my anger, and that's when I got into trouble. I've been sober for eight months and counting."

"Tonight?" Her voice came out breathy and tight, and the space between her legs felt warm and liquid with want because she hadn't had a man in her bed since him and she missed him.

No, no—she missed sex. Which was normal. She'd been cleared to resume her nonexistent sex life from the private OB/GYN—who her mother had made sign a nondisclosure form, HIPAA be damned—six weeks ago, as long as she used reliable birth control, and it had taken everything Brooke had not to laugh in the woman's face.

So she didn't necessarily miss this man. She just missed men in general.

Right.

"Ginger ale. In a beer glass." Then he brushed his lips against hers, and she was powerless to do anything but open her mouth for him. When he licked inside her, she tasted sugar and ginger, not beer.

Pop shouldn't be so seductive, but this was crazy. How did he know that was exactly what she needed to hear? How could he taste so good?

How could she still want him so damned much?

Because she did.

He broke the kiss but he didn't pull away. Somehow, they were closer now and she could feel the heat of his erection pulsing against her belly. She could feel her pulse matching his, beat for beat.

"I want to see you again," he murmured against her lips. Then his mouth was trailing over her cheek, toward her ear. "I need more than just one night, Brooke. But I won't ask you for anything else."

"Yes." The word slipped out before she could think better of it, before the logistics of another night in Flash's arms could rear their ugly head. She needed more from him, too.

"Where? Say the word and I'm there, babe. I'm anywhere you need me." As he spoke, he pressed his knee between her legs, putting pressure right where she needed it. She couldn't fight down the moan. God, it'd been so long since another person had touched her for pleasure. *Her* pleasure. "Just tell me you need me."

"My house. I need…"

But reality reared its head.

Her mother was at her house, babysitting her son. Mom didn't live with Brooke and Bean, but she did live in what the real estate agent had described as the mother-in-law house on the property, a completely separate building almost 250 yards away from the main house—close enough for baby emergencies, but not under the same roof.

However, if Brooke waltzed in with Flash on her arm, they'd never get to the bed. Mom and Flash—that was a scene Brooke wasn't ready to face tonight. Maybe not ever.

"I need half an hour before you come over." She could get Mom out of the house and give herself a chance to change her mind. Or at least make sure she had some condoms because she wasn't going to make the exact same mistake again.

A honking horn tore through the night. Flash and Brooke jerked apart just as Kyle Morgan emerged from the back of the Bluebird. Guiltily Brooke glanced at the car, where Alex glared at her, then at Flash, then back at her.

Right. They had an audience and Flash had just kissed her, and she'd probably been about twenty seconds from completely throwing herself at him.

"Hey, Brooke—everything okay?" Kyle asked, sounding meaner than she'd ever heard him. "Where's Alex?"

Flash took another step back. He looked at Brooke like he was waiting for her to lead here.

"In the car." Kyle stopped next to her, eyeing Flash with a healthy dose of warning. "This is a friend of mine."

"Great set tonight," Flash said, cutting through the awkwardness and stretching his hand toward Kyle. "Flash Lawrence. Sounds like you had some big hits waiting to happen in there. Eric Church, maybe? He could bring down stadiums with that one song about rebels."

Kyle glanced warily at Brooke before returning Flash's

handshake. "Thanks. Toby Keith was also eyeing 'My One, Her Only' for his next album."

Flash whistled appreciatively and Brooke felt Kyle relax. How did he do that? Flash Lawrence could charm his way into any situation. She'd fallen for that charm once.

She couldn't afford to fall again.

As Flash and Kyle made small talk about country singles and Flash offered his opinion on what played well at the rodeos, Brooke had to accept that somehow, Flash had known exactly what she needed to hear—that he wasn't the same man he'd been when he'd made all those awful headlines. He'd worked on being a better man.

Had he become the kind of man she'd want around her son?

Except she wasn't *just* a single mother thinking about dating again, and Bean wasn't *just* her son. He was Flash's son, too, and she couldn't keep his baby away from him, no matter what. She knew what it was like to grow up without a father. She couldn't do that to Bean. Not if Flash was willing to step up.

Was he?

"Well, it was great meeting you, Morgan," Flash said, shaking Kyle's hand again. "Looking forward to hearing your next big hit."

Kyle actually blushed at that. "Always great to hear from a fan. Will we be seeing you again soon?" He held out his hand to Flash.

Brooke didn't miss that *we*.

Flash heard it, too. He cut a glance at her as he shook Kyle's hand again. "That depends on Brooke."

Kyle leveled an intimidating look at Flash and didn't let go of his hand. Instead, he pulled Flash off balance. "You're damn right it does. Alex isn't the only one you'll have to go through if you hurt her." Then, just as quickly as it had appeared, the threat of violence dissipated into the night air.

Surprise registered on Flash's face but, after a beat, he broke out that smile Brooke saw every time Bean grinned at her. "Trust me, hurting Brooke is the last thing I'd ever want to do."

Then both men turned to her.

So this was the moment when she had to make a decision. Was letting Flash back into her life and her son's life a good idea, or was it another mistake waiting to happen?

Knowing her luck, both.

Just like Bean had been both the biggest mistake of her life and the best thing that had ever happened to her.

"Let me give you my info," she told Flash, holding out her hand for his phone. She would have preferred not to do this with Kyle standing right next to her, but this was still better than having Kyle catch them kissing.

Flash unlocked his phone and handed it to her. Her heart going a mile a minute, she put in her address and number and added the note, "half an hour" to give her enough time to get Mom out of the house and…and decide how she was going to handle Flash.

She was not bringing Flash home to have wild, crazy, *great* sex with him again. Absolutely not. This was about Bean. Her world began and ended with him now. That's all there was to it because a boy needed his father. Even if that boy was only three months old.

She handed the phone back and turned to Kyle with a studied casualness she definitely wasn't feeling. "Hey, if I need a little help on a few songs, you're interested?" Because everything on the *Roots* album was…energetic, to say the least, and Kyle was good for ballads.

Kyle's eyes lit up. "Hell, yeah, sweetheart. Just give me a call. Good meeting you, Lawrence."

But the man didn't move. He just stood there, watching her and Flash to see what was going to happen next.

"Morgan." Flash tipped his hat. "Brooke. I'll be seeing

you." He packed a hell of a lot into his gaze before he turned on his heel and strolled out of the parking lot.

She about broke out into a sweat as she watched him walk away. One thing was for sure—if anything, Flash's ass had only gotten better in the last year. A man who rode broncos and bulls for a living had the legs and backside to go with it. The first time they'd had sex—against the wall of her dressing room—he hadn't even taken his chaps off. She'd had a view of that ass in her dressing room mirror that even now threatened to make her melt.

She wasn't inviting him over for sex. She had a single-minded purpose here—informing him he was a father.

But Lord, that man made every part of her weak. Always had and, apparently, always would. She just needed to be strong enough to get through the next few hours.

Honestly, she wasn't sure she was *that* strong. Especially when he turned and tipped his hat to her, the model of the country gentleman.

"Honey," Kyle started when Flash was out of sight. "Did I just meet the inspiration for all those new songs?"

"It's not like that," she protested, and to her own ears, it sounded weak. "He's a friend."

Kyle gaped at her. Yeah, he wasn't buying it, either.

"The way he looked at you? No way. That's a man who wants a lot more than 'friendship,'" he said, throwing in air quotes for good measure. "And the way you're looking at him? Come *on*. I may be an old man, but I'm not blind."

Brooke didn't have a snappy comeback to that, but Alex saved her. "Are we going?" she all but shouted through the car window.

"Be careful!" Kyle called as Brooke climbed into the car. "And call me if you need backup!"

Yeah, like that was going to happen. She just waved as Alex sped off.

How would people like Kyle react when he found out

that she'd been sitting on the juiciest of details for months? She hoped people wouldn't be too hurt that they hadn't been important enough to be in the know, but, seriously, aside from the executives on her record label, the private OB/ GYN and nurse who'd delivered Bean at Brooke's home, the equally private pediatrician and Alex—and Mom, of course—no one else knew.

But she couldn't hide her son forever. She wanted to take him to parks and the zoo and…and just out. She wanted to talk to other moms she knew about what was normal and what wasn't. Hell, she wanted to take some pictures with Bean, not just cell phone shots. She wanted to do all the normal stuff with her son.

She didn't want to hide. Not from her friends, not from her fans and not from Flash.

Worse, when she daydreamed about all those fun things, she wasn't alone. Flash was next to her.

In her perfect world, Flash was by her side during the day and in her bed at night. Her son didn't have to grow up without his father, like Brooke had. And she didn't have to feel so alone anymore.

But that fantasy was just that—fantasy. Instead of that perfect world, she'd invited him home to tell him about Bean and also to *not* have sex with him.

The tension rolling off Alex was palatable, which had to be the only reason Brooke heard herself repeating the lie, "He's just a friend."

"Uh-huh." Yeah, Alex wasn't buying any of that as she took off for the 440.

From there, they'd take 40 west to the house she'd bought with the money her uncle had managed not to embezzle. Her home was on five fenced-in acres. If she had another hit record and successful tour, she had plans to completely renovate the sprawling mid-century ranch house. She hadn't even been able to paint the rooms while she'd been pregnant because the smell of primer had made her sick.

"The show went well, don't you think?" Brooke tried again, desperate for a subject change.

"Hon," Alex said in her growly voice, "did you tell him about Bean?"

This was the problem with best friends. There was no hiding anything from them. Because of course Alex had figured out that the one show she'd missed was the rodeo in Texas.

"No," she said, because more lies would only be an insult to Alex's intelligence.

Alex thought that over as she began to weave through traffic like the devil himself was hot on their tail. Finally she asked, "Are you going to?"

Brooke had closed her eyes. Flash was the boy's father. She simply didn't have a choice.

"Yes," she admitted, wondering why it felt like such a defeat. "But…"

"Yeah, I know—don't tell your mother," Alex grumbled. "She'll find out sooner or later."

Later, Brooke prayed. Please let it be much, much later.

Her mother had sat on the secret of Brooke's paternity for twenty-some-odd years. Brooke could keep Flash a secret for just a little bit longer.

She was going to tell Flash about Bean and hope all he'd said about not letting his anger rule him was the truth. But…

God, it was selfish and wrong, but she wanted just one more time with him before she told him she was the mother of his child.

One last grasp at the woman she'd been a year ago. A lifetime ago.

Humming a melody that built itself around the words, she had to wonder—was bringing Flash to her home another huge mistake or the making of another perfect memory?

Four

At exactly eleven forty-five, Flash walked up the front walk to Brooke's house, which was a long rancher that looked a bit shabby around the edges. The whole thing was set almost half a mile back from the road, creating the appearance of privacy. Flash didn't see any other lights and the night was hushed. He did his best to tread quietly, afraid to disturb the quiet.

Clearly, Brooke didn't want anyone to see him coming or going and he respected that—after their night together, she'd become the subject of a lot of media scrutiny.

The temptation to whistle was strong, but he tamped it down. It was a nice night and Brooke had kissed him. Sure, her new music was a broadside attack on him, but she was stunningly talented and she'd kissed him. He'd said what he needed to say and then *she'd kissed him*. She needed him and, by God, being needed was freaking amazing. This had all the markings of another amazing night.

All in all, things were looking up.

But doubt was trying to crowd out his good mood. Why did she need so much time to get ready? Possibly she just needed to pick up—as if he gave a flying rat's ass if there were dishes in the sink or clothes on the floor.

Another possibility bugged him. Because what if she needed the extra time to get rid of someone?

The thought of her being married or hustling some dude out of the house made his stomach tighten, but he breathed through the pressure. He was not the boss of Brooke. He had no claim on her whatsoever, and it'd been over a year since they'd been together.

He wanted her but not enough to ask her to cheat with him. The bonds of marriage were unbreakable. Hell, his own father still deeply mourned the loss of Flash's mother and that'd been fourteen years ago. Trixie Lawrence was still Milt's wife. Not even death would change that.

Flash would do damn near anything for another night with Brooke. But he wouldn't wreck a marriage.

Everything else, though…

Kissing Brooke Bonner again had brought it all back to him. The feel of her body flush against his, the taste of her singing on his tongue. She was honey sweet and he wanted to sip her. Just thinking about her hand on his chest, how her fingers had curled into his shirt to hold him close while he'd done his damnedest to show her how good he could be for her—he was downright giddy.

A long, painful year of "self-improvement" and "intro-spection" was behind him. All that time without women to relieve the pressure, without beer to dull the frustration. Months of reining himself in, no matter how much some jackasses deserved a punch to the mouth. Thirteen freak-ing months of watching Brooke from a distance, wonder-ing if he haunted her dreams like she haunted his—and now he was so close to having her again that it was physi-cally painful to walk.

The need to bury himself in her body beat a steady rhythm through his veins, all because she'd kissed him.

Flash had to stop just outside the circle of light cast by the porch lights and wait for his blood to cool. He wasn't expecting anything from this...*visit*. There was no way six songs worth of percolating rage had been erased with some good groveling and a kiss.

But...best case, they'd be naked at some point before dawn broke and stay that way until at least lunch tomorrow. He had a pack of condoms in his back pocket, purchased in a fit of optimism after discovering she'd be at the Bluebird. He didn't have to report in at the Bridgestone Arena before Friday afternoon. He could happily spend a few days wrapped up in Brooke.

But that was best case. Hope for the best, plan for the worst, and the worst case was Brooke taking advantage of what seemed like acres of privacy to read him the freaking riot act. Just because she'd molded her body to his and whispered, "I need you," in his ear didn't mean Flash was about to get lucky.

Failure to plan is planning to fail. He'd learned that the hard way over the last year.

So this was the plan. If she got mad, he wasn't going to get mad back. This wasn't a screaming contest and he didn't have to win. Yeah, it would suck, but he deserved to be put in his place, as his brother Oliver and brother-in-law Pete loved to remind him. He would grit his teeth, focus on breathing, take a walk if he started to lose his cool and hopefully figure out what, exactly, he'd done to inspire such passionate songwriting. Then he'd make his apologies—again—and do what he could to make things right and...

And then he'd walk away.

If that's what she wanted, that's what he'd do.

And if he had to walk away, he wouldn't go to a bar and pick a fight. He'd go pound out a few miles on a treadmill at his hotel workout room until he couldn't move.

There. That was a plan.

With his emotions firmly under control, Flash strode up the front steps.

Before he could knock, the door swung open and there she was.

"Brooke," he said, his body tightening at the sight of her.

She'd lost the vest thing and the belt, as well as the heavy jewelry that'd been around her neck. Which gave him a hell of an unobstructed view of her cleavage. But the worst thing of all was she'd lost her boots. The sight of her bare toes slammed into his gut, and he went hard when she placed one delicate little foot on top of the other. Her toes were painted a deep, sultry red, and he wanted to suck on each one until she screamed.

The space between them sparked with electricity, just like it had the first time he'd clapped eyes on this woman. There was something about her that lit him up, and he was tired of trying to ignore that elemental reaction.

She needed him. She'd asked him here. He wanted her. Simple.

He realized he was still staring at her toes. He jerked his eyes up.

Brooke stared up at him, her mouth forming a round little O. Then she dropped her gaze, blushing furiously. "Flash. You're on time."

"I would never disappoint a lady."

She tucked her lower lip under her teeth and he fought back a groan. Was she trying to torture him?

He desperately wanted to believe her hesitation was because she didn't know how to ask for what she wanted. She hadn't had any problem telling him where and how to touch her last time, and he'd done his best to give her what she'd needed. Because he wanted to give her anything she wanted. *Everything* she wanted.

And he couldn't do that outside the house, so he stepped

inside. Into her. Her head popped up, her eyes wide and dark with what he prayed was desire.

"I missed you," he said, cupping her cheeks in his hands and lifting her face to his. He didn't kiss her, but they were right back to where they'd been earlier, before they'd been interrupted. Brooke was in his arms and he didn't know how he'd get her out of his system.

"You said that."

"Well, it's true. I've never missed anyone like I missed you."

Her hand snaked up behind his neck, holding him against her. It was the sweetest thing he'd ever felt, that touch of possession. "How much?" Her voice was whisper soft as she backed up, pulling him with her.

He slid one hand down her neck, tracing the valley between her breasts before he settled it on her hip and pulled her into him. The last time he'd held her like this, she'd looped her arms around his neck and her legs around his waist and begged him to make her come. He'd done exactly as she'd asked. Twice.

"So much, babe. I'll do anything you want—you know that, right?"

Her eyelashes fluttered, the blush spreading down her neck and across her magnificent chest. He leaned down and pressed his lips against her pink skin, the warmth of her body setting his blood on fire. The last time he'd seen her breasts, he'd sucked on her rosy nipples until she'd moaned and thrashed beneath him.

Her chest heaved at his touch as her fingers curled around his neck, pulling him closer. "Anything?"

Yes—it was right there in her voice, waiting for him to come get it. Brushing his lips against her cheek, he slid both hands down her waist, around to her backside. He filled his hands with her, lifting her and pulling her against his erection. She gasped and he thought he might come right then. "*Anything*. You want me to stop, I'll stop," he murmured, pressing kisses that trailed over her skin until he could whisper in her ear. "You want me to leave, I'll leave. Just say the word."

Then he waited, the lobe of her ear resting against his lips, her bottom firm in his hands, the warmth of her breasts heating him up. This might be the last moment he could walk away from her, and it sure as hell wouldn't be a dignified walk. Every square inch of his body—a few inches in particular—throbbed to be closer to her, to pull her into his arms and hold her for as long as he could.

He felt her inhale, then let the air out slowly, her honey-sweet breath caressing over his cheek. Each second that ticked by was an eternity of torture, but he forced himself to be patient.

"Don't leave, Flash," she whispered, her lips touching his cheek. He shuddered as she leaned forward, bringing her body completely flush with his, and kissed his neck. "Stay."

Then she bit him—not hard, but with enough pressure to take everything that was already throbbing in his body and kick it into overdrive.

She didn't have to ask twice. He kicked the door shut behind him and spun her around. Her back hit the door with a muffled thud and then Flash was kissing her, her sweetness overwhelming his senses, her body erasing everything but this moment.

He squeezed her ass and ground his aching erection against her, and, God help him, he couldn't get enough. He closed a hand around one of her breasts, letting the heavy weight fill his palm.

She sank one hand into his hair, knocking his hat off. With the other, she grabbed his hand and jerked it away from her breast at the same time she pulled his head back.

"Shh!" she hissed, real fear in her eyes. "Quiet!"

"What is it, babe? What's wrong?" He swallowed and, holding himself in check, did the right thing. "We can stop. We don't…"

Shaking her head *no*, Brooke released his hand and stroked her thumb over his cheek. "I don't want to stop but…it's complicated, that's all."

"Just so we're clear—you're not married?" She shook her head *no* again and he almost sagged in relief. "Engaged?"

She gave him the saddest of smiles, one that did some mighty funny things to his heart. "No. Just… I need you, Flash. Like before." Her voice was barely a whisper, something he felt more than he heard. "But you have to be quiet and don't touch my breasts."

He gave her a strange look—if he was remembering correctly, she'd absolutely loved it when he'd played with her breasts.

"Please," she said softly, pulling him back down to her. "Just one more time, like it used to be. And afterwards… I'll understand, no matter what happens."

He stared at her. What the hell was going on? He was missing something, and he couldn't tell if it was *bad* or *really bad*.

"Babe," he said, hoping to reassure her, and he made damn sure to do it quietly. "If another night—or another weekend is what you need—that's what I want, too." He touched his forehead to hers. "Just tell me."

Breathing hard, she didn't reply right away. Then her beautiful green eyes fluttered open, and even before she spoke, Flash knew what her answer would be.

Yes.

He covered her mouth with a hard kiss, stuck in between this exact moment right now and an almost identical one last year. This is what he wanted—Brooke pressed against him, her mouth opening for his, her teeth scraping his lip.

She dug her fingernails into his scalp, the flash of pain burning bright into pleasure.

Oh, yeah—she pushed him and tormented him like no other woman ever had and he loved it.

Then she jerked her head away from his. "Condoms," she hissed, her voice soft but serious. *"Now."*

"Bed?" he asked, reaching to get the packet from his back pocket.

"No—can't wait." While he struggled with the foil wrapper on the condom, she went to work on his belt buckle.

God, she really couldn't wait.

He groaned as her fingers closed around him, and he almost dropped the condom when she stroked up, then down.

"I missed you too, Flash," she said, her mouth at his neck again. "No one makes me feel the way you do."

Then her teeth scraped over his skin and she squeezed him, and if he had been able to think right now, he might pause to break that statement down. But he couldn't think, couldn't do anything but feel her hands on him, feel the warmth of her breasts pressing against his chest.

She needed him. It was a hell of a thing.

Somehow, he got the condom on and got her skirt lifted. Thank goodness she had on a thin pair of panties. Flash didn't even bother to pull them down. He just shoved them aside and positioned himself at her entrance. The smell of her sex hit his nose like a bomb going off, and he groaned again.

"Now," Brooke breathed in his ear, hitching one leg over his hip. "Now, Flash. Now, now *now…*"

He slid his hands under her ass to lift her and then, with one thrust, he sank into her wet heat.

"Oh," she moaned, and he swallowed that sound with another kiss.

For a moment, he couldn't do anything but stand there as sensations swamped him.

For a year he'd been trying to forget how right she felt surrounding him, how perfectly they fit together.

It hadn't worked.

He couldn't forget what they had together, this electric physical connection.

"Brooke," he said, his words coming out a strangled whisper. He touched his forehead to hers and stared down into her eyes. He desperately wanted to believe he saw his own desire reflected back at him. "Oh, *Brooke*."

"Shh." Then she was kissing him with all the passion he remembered from last year, all the pent-up desire that had been driving him slowly mad.

He began to rock into her, each thrust threatening to destroy him anew—especially when she whispered, "More," in his ear before she bit down on his lobe.

"Yes, ma'am," he whispered back.

It'd been like this in her dressing room, hard and fast and quiet against the door because people were right out in the hallway. It'd been exciting then. It was still exciting.

He paused long enough to shift his grip on her bottom, lifting her up and bracing his feet so he could support her with one hand. With the other, he reached down between their bodies to where they were joined. Brooke's head dropped back, her chest heaving as Flash pinched the folds of skin right above where he was buried inside of her.

Beneath his touch, her body shuddered. Her head thrashed against the door and he felt the spasms of her orgasm begin to move around him, clenching him so, *so* tight. A low roaring sound filled the air around them as he came and she came, too. It was only after that he realized the roaring was him, groaning in pure bliss.

He collapsed against her body, pinning her to the door, still inside of her. Breathing hard, he couldn't think, couldn't talk.

Home.

That was the only word he had, one that repeated itself over and over again when Brooke kissed his neck, then his mouth.

This was what coming home felt like.

Which was wrong. She wasn't home. He followed the rodeo. This was just…one of those things. A good night. Maybe a great week.

He pulled free of her body but not her arms. "Babe," he murmured against her hair, but then he stopped because he wasn't sure what was going to come out of his mouth next.

"I'm so sorry," Brooke whispered, and he heard the catch in her voice.

He reared back, staring down at her. No, he wasn't imagining things—she was on the verge of tears. "Don't apologize to me, Brooke. You and I…"

But that was when a new sound reached his ears—something high-pitched, almost a whine. Something that sent a shiver of real fear racing down his back.

A single tear spilled over and ran down Brooke's cheek. "So, *so* sorry," she whispered, slipping out from under his arm and leaving him hanging—literally. "I didn't want it to be this way."

"Brooke?" He turned but she was already halfway up the stairs. Her skirt had already fallen back down and she didn't look like she'd just changed his world.

And she didn't stop.

"Brooke!" he said as the noise got louder, grating over his nerves like sandpaper. "What—"

"We woke the baby," she said, choking on the words.

"The baby? What *baby*?" Flash stared up at her, the hairs on his arms standing at full attention, like lightning was about to strike.

Someone else's baby. That was the only thing that made sense. Not hers. Not…

Oh, God.

She made it to the top of the stairs and still hadn't answered.

"Brooke," he shouted. *"Whose baby?"*

"Mine." She turned around then and looked down at him, crying hard. "And yours. Our baby, Flash. *Our son.*"

Then she turned and ran.

Five

"Oh, Bean," Brooke murmured, scooping the baby into her arms. "Momma needed just a few more minutes." Five more minutes to break it to Flash that his son was upstairs. Five more minutes to untangle her body from his.

But it wasn't meant to be.

The baby howled his displeasure, and Brooke quickly realized what the problem was. He was soaking wet and probably hungry, too. He'd already been asleep when she'd gotten home.

Everything was wrong. That wasn't how she'd wanted to tell Flash. It wasn't fair to just drop that bomb on him. Not mere seconds after he'd been inside of her. Not when her legs were still shaking with the force of the orgasm he'd unleashed.

She hadn't planned to have sex with him again. No, that was a lie because obviously, she *had*—God, he was still so good—but she'd resolved to do the right thing and tell him about Bean first. And that resolve had lasted all of thirty-seven seconds. Right until he'd touched her.

She handed Bean his rattle shaped like a frog that croaked when he shook it. He only got to play with that toy when she was changing him and Bean was endlessly fascinated with it. Thankfully, it worked and the baby quieted down as she got him cleaned up.

That was when she realized the house was silent. Too quiet.

Was Flash still here? Or had he opened that door and walked out of her house and her life? Oh, Lord. Not that she would blame him for that, because she couldn't. She'd hidden Bean from him. An entire pregnancy, a birth, *a baby*—and she hadn't breathed a word of it to him. Really, that was unforgivable.

If Flash walked, that didn't change anything. She was still responsible for Bean, just like she'd always been. But now that Flash knew, she wasn't going to hide the baby anymore. It was time to show the world she had an amazing little boy. She'd tell her mother and her record label that she was going public and that was *that*. Her next album would get some extra PR, so everyone would win.

Brooke focused on the job before her. One day at a time and, when that didn't work, one hour at a time.

The sound of heavy tread on steps ricocheted through her body like a gunshot, and she gasped. The baby began to fuss again.

Flash hadn't left. Instead, he was coming upstairs. Somehow, that was worse.

Breathe. She had to breathe. It was good Flash hadn't left. Yay, he wasn't abandoning them! That was great, right?

Then he was standing in the doorway, staring at her with his mouth open and his eyes bugging out of his head, white as a ghost. He didn't say anything. She wasn't sure he was breathing.

This felt like something out of a nightmare, the reoccurring one she'd had after she'd realized she was pregnant, had looked Flash up and seen all those news stories. A shiver of panic raced down her back as she remembered everything she'd read—the drunken bar fights, the criminal charges for assault.

But as she stared at Flash staring at her, she knew she wanted more than just a fight-or-flight reaction out of Flash, more than sex against the door.

Well. The show had to go on, didn't it? She picked up Bean and turned to Flash. "Can you hold him?"

His mouth shut, then opened. "What?" The word sounded like she'd tortured it out of him.

"Here." She held Bean out to Flash. "This is Bean." She swallowed. "James Frasier Bonner, but I call him Bean."

She wouldn't have thought it possible, but Flash got even paler as he stared at the baby in her arms.

"He's yours," she said. "Please, Flash. I have to change his sheets and wash my hands. Can you hold him? For just a minute?"

Bean seemed to notice Flash for the first time. His little body went stiff and he made a noise of concern. On instinct, Brooke tucked her son into her arms. "It's okay," she murmured, watching Flash over the top of Bean's head. "It's…" she swallowed. "That's Daddy, baby. That's your father."

"You… I…" Flash stuttered. Then, without another word, he spun on his heel and was gone.

It felt like a punch to the gut, but before Brooke could do anything but stiffen in pain, he returned, his eyes blazing. "I am coming back," he said, his voice quiet and level and, somehow, all the more unsettling for it. Then he was gone again. This time, she heard his footsteps thundering down the stairs.

She hurried to the doorway. "Flash?" she called after him. Was it a good thing that he was coming back?

He stopped when he got to the bottom of the stairs, his back to her. His hands were definitely clenching and unclenching. He looked like he'd just been bucked off a bronco a half second too early to win it all.

"I need a minute," he said. The look he shot her over his shoulder made her stumble back, it was that intense. "Just give me a damned minute, Brooke."

He straightened and walked out the front door. At least he didn't slam it. That had to count for something, right?

Brooke had a baby.
Brooke had *his* baby.
He had a baby.

Flash paced relentlessly around his truck, struggling to breathe. The old Flash would've probably already punched the side of the truck a few times, breaking his hand and denting the metal. It was a pointless, destructive way of coping with a problem, striking out like that.

He'd thought she'd been giving him the gift of forgiveness with her kiss, her touch, her body.

And the whole time, the baby had been upstairs.

Jesus, he and Brooke had a baby *together*.

How old?

Flash did the math and, oddly, counting months helped him breathe. Thirteen months. Babies took nine months, right? No, wait—Renee, his sister-in-law, had been pregnant for ten months. So thirteen minus nine and a half, just to be safe, meant that baby boy was…

Three, maybe four months old.

Flash's knees threatened to buckle, and he had to hang on to the side of the truck bed just to keep from collapsing. He had a son who was almost four months old already and he hadn't known.

Because Brooke hadn't told him.

The world went a deep, crimson red at the edges again at what he'd missed—the first heartbeat, the labor and delivery, his son's first breath, first smile, first *everything*. All those moments, gone. He'd never get them back. All because Brooke hadn't told him, goddammit.

That was unforgivable.

But the moment the thought crossed his mind, Flash pushed back at it. He had to reframe this right *now*, because he was many things but he didn't like to think *stupid* was one of them.

He was angry, yes. Flash let the anger flow but he didn't try to hold on to it. He let it pass him by and forced himself to look underneath. Before he'd started court-mandated anger management therapy, he never would have thought there was more to anger than good old-fashioned rage, but he knew better now.

For starters, he was surprised. Not that *surprised* was a strong enough word, but it'd have to do. Brooke hadn't told him and then the baby had been crying, and Flash had been *stunned*—and that was a perfectly normal reaction to discovering a one-night stand had a child that was his.

What the hell did he know about being a father?

He'd gone over to his brother Oliver's house and played with his niece, Trixie, but that didn't mean he was qualified to be a father. He rode bulls and wild broncos for a living and did stupid stuff like having one-night stands. Not exactly the kind of thing a good dad did.

He didn't know how long he paced in circles, but eventually the world went back to being plain old dark.

He paused and looked up at Brooke's house. One light was on in what might be the baby's room. No, Flash couldn't keep thinking of that child as "the baby." That boy had a name. He was James Frasier Bonner, which was a good, strong name—even if she had given the boy Flash's real, awful name. James could be a Jim or a Jimmy or even a Jamie—*never* a Frasier.

What had Brooke called him? Bean? What the hell kind of nickname was that, anyway?

He took comfort in the fact that he must have been right—she'd tried to look him up and found those headlines and seen the pictures and decided it was safer for her and her child if Flash wasn't around. That was the only thing that made sense. He understood that on a rational level. It was a good thing that she'd do anything to protect their son.

But that didn't change the fact that *she hadn't told him*. She'd kept his son away from him. She'd never even given Flash a chance to show he had what it took to be a good father.

He would not let his anger get the better of him, but, by God, he had no idea how he was supposed to forgive her for what she'd done.

Forgiveness could come later. Right now, he had to make sure that Brooke never again managed to hide his son from him. That boy was his just as much as he was hers.

Brooke was the mother of his child.

He knew what he had to do.

He pulled out his phone. Brooke probably wasn't going to like this, but that was too damn bad, wasn't it? He wasn't about to try to handle a situation of this magnitude by himself. God only knew that'd be a disaster. Something like this required finesse and PR skills, not to mention a sensitive touch. None of those things would ever describe Flash, in this life or the next.

But they did describe his sister, Chloe.

He got voice mail and, scowling, hit Redial. He knew Chloe and her husband, Pete, were already in Nashville. They always got in a few days early to get everything set up for the All-Around All-Stars Rodeo. Finally, on the third try, Chloe answered and said in a breathless voice, "This better be important, Flash."

He cringed, trying not to think about what he'd interrupted. "Sis," he began, but the words, *I have a son with Brooke* got stuck in his throat.

Not that Chloe would've listened anyway. "I swear to

God, if you're in jail, I'm going to leave you to rot this time," she snapped.

In the background, Flash heard Chloe's husband, Pete Wellington, growl, "Now what's he done?"

Well, sometimes she had finesse. "Go to hell," Flash muttered. "I am having a legitimate problem and I thought I could count on you, but if you both are going to treat me like I'm a child, I'll do this myself." He hung up and then had to walk around the damn truck a few more times.

Yeah, he'd done more than enough to screw up his own life in the past. He knew that. Hell, everyone knew that. But since he'd started therapy, he would've thought he'd demonstrated that he was serious about being a better man. But maybe Chloe would always see a failure when she looked at him and, frankly, Flash didn't have the time or space to deal with that. Especially not right now.

He hadn't gotten far when his phone rang. Chloe. If he wasn't desperate he'd ignore her, but…

"Sorry," he gritted out. Chloe had always been the one to bail him out before, and he knew she hated it. "I'm not in jail or drunk. Not in a bar."

"What's wrong?" At least now she sounded concerned. And, oddly, that was what Flash needed.

"If I send you an address—a house—can you and Pete be here in…" He mentally calculated how long it'd take them to get from the hotel next to the Bridgestone arena in downtown Nashville to Brooke's house. "In twenty minutes? Quietly, without attracting any attention?"

After all, Flash hadn't known about his son because no one did. James Frasier Bonner hadn't shown up on any social media or paparazzi site. Brooke had gone dark months ago. Probably about the time she'd been unable to hide her pregnancy anymore.

"Flash," Chloe said, and finally she sounded about

right for this situation—worried, a little scared. "What's going on?"

He looked up at that lit window, where the one woman he couldn't forget was holding a son he hadn't known he had. This was how it had to be.

"I have a baby."

Chloe gasped, a noise of pure pain. Flash could hear Pete in the background saying, "Hon? You okay?" Belatedly, Flash remembered that Chloe had been trying to get pregnant for months now with no luck.

"Sorry, sis. I just found out. And I need help."

"Yes." He could hear her pulling herself back together. "Yes, of course we'll help. Who's..." She swallowed nervously. "Who's the mother?"

He looked up at the window again. Brooke was standing there, James Frasier Bonner in her arms. She'd always been the most beautiful woman he'd ever seen, but there was something about the image she presented, his son resting his head against her breast, her arms holding the baby tight—there was something right about it.

Why hadn't she told him? Damn it all to hell.

"It's Brooke. Brooke Bonner had my son."

He exhaled slowly. He was going to make things right, starting *now*.

Six

What was he doing out there?

Flash appeared to be pacing around his truck, which was hopefully an improvement over the way he'd all but bolted out of the house like the hounds of hell were nipping at his heels.

It was a good sign, she decided as she quickly washed up. He hadn't driven off in a blind fury, and even though he'd obviously been upset—what a pitifully weak word *that* was—he hadn't done anything…scary.

God, this was a freaking mess. She was nauseous with worry. For crying out loud, she could face down an arena filled with fifty thousand screaming fans with little more than a few butterflies in her stomach, but one man was going to be her undoing.

As if he could sense her panic, Bean looked up at her from where she'd set him down on the rug and smiled like he was trying to reassure her. He had his father's charm, but Bean's drooly grin was all sweetness and innocence, whereas Flash's grins promised wonderful, dangerous things. Things like long nights in hotels and hot sex against the door.

Brooke clung to that innocent baby grin. "Oh, you're having a grand time, aren't you?" she cooed to him as she swept him into her arms. "All sorts of excitement happening here tonight, and none of it involves sleeping."

Bean gurgled appreciatively and Brooke kissed his little head. At least someone was having fun.

Bean in her arms, she peeked out the window. Flash was still out there, leaning against the side of the truck. Wait—was he on his phone? Oh, hell.

Just then Flash glanced up, and even through the dark and distance, she *felt* the moment their gazes locked.

Who was he talking to? This could be a disaster. Of course there was a contingency plan for when she announced Bean's existence and, knowing her publicist, there was one for if the information leaked. She didn't want Bean to be gossip. She wanted to be the one controlling the information. She wanted to introduce her son to the world.

She could still get in front of this. She was supposed to meet with the publicist about tonight's show and approve a series of small shows on Music Row in downtown Nashville until the album officially dropped. Then there was a tour that was already set up, even though it hadn't been announced yet. She had to go over the album the final time with the producers. And then there were the interviews—so far, all by phone.

They might have to spend all that time talking about her one big mistake instead of her album, but she was going to control this narrative, by God.

With or without Flash.

Would he acknowledge the baby publicly? Would he sign off on the inevitable PR that would go along with introducing Bean to the world?

Or was this about to be a fight?

She didn't want a fight. She didn't want to be on opposite sides of Flash, stuck in a tug-of-war with the baby as the rope. She wanted Flash on her side.

Especially since Brooke was going to have to tell her mother about him. At the rate things were going, Brooke would have to tell her soon. Like, in a day or two. God help her, Brooke didn't want to.

Flash Lawrence was the sum total of things Crissy Bonner hated and Brooke knew it. Crissy would do the exact same thing Brooke had done—she'd start by researching Flash, and the moment those headlines came up it'd be all over.

It wouldn't matter how much Flash would claim he'd changed. Crissy Bonner would see only the irresponsible, immature ass who'd knocked her daughter up and abandoned her to brawl in bars and ride bulls—all of which put the carefully crafted career Crissy had been arranging since Brooke had turned five in danger of collapsing under the weight of scandal. Brooke didn't know anything about her father, who Mom claimed had split when Brooke was still crawling. But, needless to say, Crissy Bonner was not a big fan of any man who abandoned a woman and a child.

Nope. None of that was *for the best*.

Cuddling Bean to her chest, Brooke settled into the rocker. No matter what, her son came first. She and Flash would…work something out. Shared custody, maybe. Brooke wouldn't allow her mother or her record label or anyone—not even Flash himself—to hurt her child.

But what if there could be something more? For the first time since Bean had announced himself to Flash, Brooke's thoughts turned not to what'd happened months ago or what was going to happen tomorrow, but to those last few moments before it'd all gone to hell.

Flash, pressing her back against the door. Flash, kissing her even better than she'd remembered. Flash, bringing her to orgasm like no time at all had passed between this night and the one thirteen months ago.

Flash, reminding her who she'd been before she'd become a mother.

She shuddered, her body tightening almost painfully with need. She didn't know how this would work—would they date? Be co-parents? It seemed pretty obvious that she couldn't spend any time with Flash without having hot, *great* sex. She was too aware of him, too needy for him. So could they be co-parents with benefits, maybe? She'd be okay with that. Bean could spend time with his father, and she could keep Flash in her bed.

Anything more seemed unlikely—he'd be chasing the rodeo and she was supposed to go on tour. They'd rarely be in the same town at the same time, much less in the same state.

Of course, that all depended on if he was calling his lawyer or the press or, hell, his girlfriend, didn't it?

She stared down at Bean, his eyes already half closed as he held on to her thumb with his tiny fingers, nursing happily. She'd never been away from her son for longer than a few hours, recording her album in between nursing him. She wanted her son to know his father, she really did. It pained her to think of him missing that part of his life, his history. She had no idea who her father's people were. Her mom had erased any trace of that man from the record.

She wouldn't allow that to happen for Bean. She was *not* going to turn into her mother.

But she couldn't bear the thought of a custody battle with Flash, couldn't even consider the idea that she might lose her son.

Brooke made her decision.

She wouldn't ask for anything more from Flash than he was willing to give, and she wouldn't let him reject his son. And there was no way in hell she would let him take the boy away from her.

She might have dozed, she couldn't tell. The next thing she knew, Flash was sitting on the footstool before her, staring at where Bean was still barely latched on.

Flash didn't look mad. If anything, he looked…focused. He wasn't pale and that wild look was gone from his eyes. When he glanced up at her, that ghost of a smile played over his lips, and she felt a smile of her own answer his.

"I'll put him down, then we can talk," she whispered. Flash nodded. She moved Bean to her shoulder and gently patted his back. Flash studied her every move with an intensity that sent little shivers down her back. When she pushed to her feet, he stood with her.

She put Bean on his back in the crib and stared down at her perfect little boy, clinging to what might be the last moment of peace for a while. The moment she left this room, things would change—quickly.

Then Flash stepped up next to her, shoulders touching, his hip warm against hers, his fingers brushing hers on the crib rail. She fought the urge to wrap her arm around his waist and lean into him.

This was what she wanted, this closeness. This feeling of being part of a team. Yeah, she had Alex and her mother, but it wasn't the same. Only Flash could seduce her with that smile, make her feel like he did.

But it was an illusion, one shattered when he leaned over and said against her ear, "We need talk. *Now.*"

She nodded and, after leaning over to brush her fingers over the baby's forehead, headed down to the library. At least, that's what she called the room, because it's where all the books were, as well as her piano. It was mostly where she went when she needed a little peace and quiet to write, because the library was on the complete opposite side of the house from Bean's room. If there had to be shouting, hopefully they wouldn't wake the baby back up.

Flash didn't follow her at first. She turned back to see him lean over the crib, a look of what she hoped was adoration on his face as he touched Bean's forehead almost the exact same way Brooke had.

"Sleep for Mommy, little man," he whispered, and if it were possible to fall in love with him in a moment, she might have done so because Flash was going to love Bean, and the baby would know his father and everything would work out.

A vision of a happy family assembled itself in her mind's eye, one where Flash got up with Bean when he fussed at night and kissed her awake in the morning. A lifetime of teaching Bean to walk and swim and ride horses, of singing along to her songs when they came on the radio and watching Flash ride from the bleachers at the rodeo. She wanted it all with him, everything that went into being a family—first steps and first words, first *everything*.

And when Bean went to bed, she wanted Flash waiting up for her after a show or coming home to her after a rodeo, celebrating his win and her hits with hot kisses and hotter sex. A lifetime of losing themselves in each other, where the sex only got better and Flash was a man she could count on, through good times and bad. Where she was the only woman he needed or wanted.

Then Flash turned to her and another icy shiver raced down her back. That intensity was still there, but anything sweet or adoring was long gone.

Say something romantic. She didn't miss that the other chorus line—*Don't say something romantic*—had disappeared completely. She couldn't stop the melody from running through her head, couldn't stop wishing Flash would hear the same song.

But it wasn't meant to be because even if Flash wasn't

throw-things-against-the-wall mad, it was obvious he was still freaking furious.

Right. Best get this over with.

She headed down the stairs, determined to hash this out. She could like him and she could want him, but she wasn't going to torpedo her career or risk her son's happiness to soothe over Flash's ruffled feathers. He could just be mad. She would protect her family.

By the time she reached the bottom of the stairs, Flash caught up with her. He grabbed her hand, as if he were afraid she might bolt. "How old?" he asked softly, even as his fingers were as hard as steel around hers.

He was hard and soft all at once, intense and gentle. She wanted to lean into him, but she wasn't entirely sure she could trust that he wouldn't push her away.

"He'll be four months next Wednesday. In here," she replied, leading him into the library. "I was in labor the night of the Grammys. I had him at three in the morning."

"Ah. I wondered why you weren't there." Flash guided her to the long blue couch arranged in front of the fireplace, but instead of sitting next to her he moved to the mantel. "Did everything go okay? Any…" He swallowed, looking ill. "Any problems for you or him?"

"No. Labor was long and not fun, but everyone was fine. Seven pounds, six ounces, all his fingers and toes. The doctors say he's right where he should be."

Flash slumped against the mantel in relief. "Good. That's good. I wish I'd been there for you."

"I wish you had been, too."

Flash stared down at the floor. "Was I right earlier? You looked me up and found the headlines?"

Her cheeks blazed with heat, but the hell of it was, she had no idea why she was embarrassed. "I did. I'm sorry, Flash. I—"

"Don't apologize." His voice was harder now. "I brought

that on myself, as my sister is so fond of reminding me." He closed his eyes and another few moments passed. Was this normal for him? She should know—but she didn't because every time she was around him, they wound up having sex instead of deep, meaningful conversations.

"Just for the record," he began suddenly in a low voice, "if I walk out of the room, it's because I don't want to lose my temper, not because I'm walking away from you. I'll come back when I'm in control because we are nowhere *near* done, Brooke."

Honest to God, she had no idea if that was a threat or a promise. "All right." She shifted nervously, trying to find something to do with her hands. She wished she could go sit at her baby grand piano and let her fingers work out a melody. She thought better when she let the music carry away her anxiety.

"Are you mad at me?" she asked. As if that answer wasn't obvious.

"I am extremely upset," he said, his voice oddly level. His eyes closed again, and he exhaled for a long moment before going on, "I am mad at you because you didn't tell me about my son. I am mad at myself because I know we used protection, but obviously it failed and I failed you. Repeatedly. I obviously wasn't as careful with your health as I should've been, and I wasn't the kind of person who you thought you could trust."

Wait—was he not throwing her under the bus here? Was he taking *responsibility*? At least some of it? "I don't blame you for this, Flash. We used condoms, but it takes two to tango."

He nodded curtly, which was the only way she knew he'd heard her. "I've learned that, for me, anger is a catch-all for my emotions, and it takes work to understand the other things I'm feeling. I am *damned* hurt right now. And surprised and a little scared and...*mad*. Because how could you hide him from me, Brooke? How could you not even give me a chance?"

His voice had begun to approach a shout, but he checked himself and began to pace in a tight circle in front of the mantel. She was reminded of an unbroken horse in a corral, running back and forth and trying to decide if it was going to charge the fence or not.

Would he bolt? Or would he settle?

"I was going to tell you," she explained.

"When?" he snapped. "Because that baby's well past newborn, Brooke."

She winced. She hated this guilt, but he was right. "I always meant to tell you, but it was easy to put off contacting you until tomorrow and tomorrow and tomorrow, and the longer I didn't tell you, the more I was afraid that you'd…"

"That I'd punch a wall or wrap my truck around a light pole?"

She winced at the truth of that. "No one else knows about him except Alex, my mother and a few medical professionals, all of whom signed nondisclosure agreements in addition to their legal obligations to keep my medical history private. Oh, and a few record executives, all who had a vested interest in keeping the news quiet."

Confusion flitted across his face. "Why, though? Are you ashamed of him?"

"Of course not." Brooke slumped back against the couch. Suddenly she was tired. She'd done a show tonight and hooked up with Flash, and now had to defend the choices she'd made during the most stressful moments of the last year. Of her *life*. "It's because I wouldn't tell anyone who you were. Not a single person knows you're Bean's father—or knew. Alex figured it out tonight. I never wanted to keep this a secret, but I got overruled by literally everyone else, all because I didn't want to bring you into it."

His eyes bugged out. "You didn't tell anyone about me?"

"You were my secret. Those headlines…" She shuddered. "Because I wouldn't identify you, my mother and my record label decided to keep the pregnancy quiet."

"Damn it," he growled, but at least he growled quietly. "I was following your career and you suddenly fell off the map and I had no idea. If I'd known, I…" He stopped and suddenly paced to the doorway, but he didn't walk out. Instead, he turned back around. He looked tortured and it hurt her.

She'd made the best of a bad situation, but she'd never stopped second-guessing herself. And the fact that he wasn't screaming and blaming her for getting pregnant in the first place—that was what she'd feared. And what she'd expected, to be honest, after reading all those headlines.

His response gave her hope. Maybe this could work. Somehow.

She went to him, resting her hand on his arm. His eyes softened as he cupped her cheek with his hand and stroked her skin with his thumb. "I wish it'd been different," she whispered, leaning into his touch. "I'm so sorry, Flash. I'd change the past if I could but…"

"Neither of us can."

Somehow, she and Flash were getting closer. His arm slid around her waist and her head rested on his shoulder. God, it felt so damn good. This was who she wanted—Flash at his best.

"He's such a great baby, Flash. I want him to know his whole family—your family."

"I called my sister," he told her. "Chloe—remember meeting her at the Fort Worth rodeo?" Brooke nodded and Flash went on, his arms tightening around her waist. "She and her husband Pete run the All-Stars and they're in town. They're heading over."

"That's fine. Chloe seemed nice."

Actually, Chloe had been more than a little upset with

Brooke because hooking up with Flash had made Brooke late to start her show. But Brooke couldn't hold that against the woman. The show had to go on, after all. If someone had to be the first to find out about Bean, it was probably for the best that it was family.

Flash snorted. "She's a bossy know-it-all, but she's saved my butt more times than I can count. And she loves babies."

"That's nice. I…" Swallowing nervously, she tilted her head back and stared up at Flash. It was wonderful that this conversation about the past wasn't a fight, but that didn't mean a discussion of the future would be easy. Especially as his fingers stroked over her skin again, warm and encouraging. Brooke got the words out before his touch distracted her. Again. "I want to make this right. I don't know if you realize this, but to this day my own mother won't tell me who my father is, and I refuse to let my own son grow up like I did. I want us do this parenting thing together."

He took several long breaths, but he didn't close his eyes, didn't walk out of the room and he wasn't yelling—so this was all progress, right? Instead, he pulled her closer, her chest flush against his. Languid heat began to build in her body because even though she was exhausted and relieved and so, *so* thankful that Flash was finally here and it was all going to be okay, she'd had all of one orgasm in months and she selfishly wanted more. With this man—no one else.

Say something romantic, she silently begged him as she molded her body against his. Something sweet and hot that would let her know it would all work out just fine. Something that would take this perfect melody between them and make it into a song.

He didn't. He didn't kiss her or offer to hold her for the few short hours of sleep she might get before Bean woke up hungry. Instead, something in his eyes hardened as his arms crushed her against him. When he spoke, his voice was silky smooth and it sent a chill down her spine.

"We're absolutely in this together from now on. That's why we'll get married as soon as possible."

Seven

"What?"

Flash didn't miss the way Brooke's body went stiff in his arms. "Married," he repeated, feeling his blood pressure rise. "As soon as possible. That boy is a Lawrence by blood and by right."

Brooke moved but, instead of curling into him, she twisted out of his grasp. "Flash—what are you *talking* about?"

Not that he expected Brooke to start jumping for joy or anything, but hadn't she just said they were in this together?

"We need to get hitched," he said. "Quickly. Tomorrow, even."

Brooke stared at him with a look of horror on her face. "No. Absolutely not."

No? *No?*

Obviously, they needed to make this legal, especially if she was going to announce *their* baby to the world at large.

"This is nonnegotiable, Brooke. You can't keep pretending that I don't exist because it's convenient for you. That's my son, by God, and I won't let you keep him from me. You *will* marry me!" he yelled.

"I have no intention of keeping your son from you," she shouted back.

Oh, if that didn't just take the cake. "More than you already have, you mean?"

A little of the shock bled into fury as her eyes flashed with righteousness. "We are *not* getting married, Flash. Under *any* circumstance."

She couldn't have hit him harder if she'd actually punched him. He had to grab on to the door frame to hold himself up.

"The hell we aren't," he snapped. "That's my son and we're good in bed—against the door—together. Why wouldn't we get married?"

Dimly, he was aware that probably wasn't the best way to phrase it but, damn it, he was *pissed*. This was not complicated. Brooke was the mother of his child and he liked her. Simple.

Her cheeks blazing, her mouth opened for what looked like a blistering response, but just then headlights flashed through the parlor, cutting her off. They both turned toward the windows as the sound of doors slamming filled the air.

Brooke went to push past him but he grabbed her arm. "This conversation isn't over," he said, trying to make it sound nice and gentle.

But the way her eyes flashed a warning and the way she jerked out of his touch made it plenty clear he hadn't succeeded. "I will *not* be forced into anything I don't want," she said, her tone icy.

Then the doorbell pealed through the house. "Oh, no— the baby!" she said, making a break for the door. "Come inside—quietly," she said to Chloe and Pete, but it was too late because that was when James Frasier Bonner decided he needed to be part of the festivities.

"Oh, I'm so sorry," Chloe Lawrence said in a quiet voice,

even though they were way past whispering. James began to wail. "We didn't mean to wake him!"

"My bad," Pete Wellington said, whipping his hat off his head. "I rang the bell. Didn't think."

Brooke heaved a mighty sigh even as she launched a forgiving smile at Chloe and Pete. "It's okay. Things haven't been exactly *quiet* here tonight," she added, shooting a look at Flash that was part challenge, part scold and all mad.

Was she going to blame this on him? He hadn't been the only one yelling! "With good reason," he shot back, crossing his arms over his chest and trying not to glare. Given the way Pete frowned at him, Flash was pretty sure he hadn't succeeded with that whole not-glaring thing.

But then again, neither had Brooke. "You'll excuse me," she said, her voice tight. "I need to go see to *my* son."

"*Our* son," Flash snapped.

Chloe and Pete took in the tension, shared a look and then moved like a calf-roping team with years of competitions under their belts. "I'll come with you, if that's okay? I can't wait to meet this little guy, even if he's grumpy," Chloe said gently, putting an arm around Brooke's shoulders and turning her toward the stairs. "I'm sure it's been a long night—for all of you."

"You have *no* idea," Brooke said, almost sagging into Chloe. Even through the haze of emotions he was barely keeping in check, Flash heard the sheer exhaustion in her voice.

Well, if that wasn't enough to make a man feel like crap.

But before he could open his mouth—regardless of what was going to come out of it—Pete advanced on him, crowding him back into the room where Flash and Brooke had ended up before.

"How's it going?" the man had the nerve to ask, his hands up as if he were ready to give Flash a hard shove should the need arise.

"Great. Freaking great. Thanks for asking," Flash said. Okay, *snarled*.

He turned and began to pace around the couch. The one where Brooke had sat and said things about understanding and co-parenting, and why, for the love of everything holy, was she so hell-bent on not getting married? Was it marriage in general? Or was it just *him*?

It wasn't like he wanted to get married. He rode the rodeo. He lived out of his suitcase ten months out of the year and rarely saw his own home. That wasn't a lifestyle that lent itself to raising an infant. And this was the year he would win it all. He was off his suspension for fighting, he was sober and focused, and he did not have time to settle down. He'd make time, damn it, because that's what family did. But if he wasn't extremely careful about how this played out, he could kiss his championship year goodbye.

Damn it all to hell. If Brooke had told him about the baby months ago, he could've spent the off season getting to know his son and making plans. Now he had to scramble—and rely on Pete Wellington, of all people, to help him out.

Flash hadn't punched a single person in months—not since he'd gotten into a brawl with his father, his brother Oliver and Pete over Pete's underhanded tactics to win the All-Stars and Chloe away from the Lawrence family. And even then, Flash hadn't been as mad as he was right now. The last time he'd felt this dangerous had been...

It'd been when Tex McGraw had said those things about Brooke and Flash had been booted off the All-Stars as a result of the fight.

"What happened?" Pete kept his voice calm and level, but he wasn't inspiring anything calm or levelheaded in Flash.

"She had my baby and didn't tell me! Come on, Wellington—keep up!" Flash realized his hands were fists now, swinging loosely at his sides as he stalked Pete around the room. He was primed to throw a punch. God, it'd feel so good to just let go…

But Pete had been around Flash long enough that this outburst didn't faze him. "You need to hit something?"

"You volunteering?"

"Jackass," Pete said easily, dancing just out of reach. "Here." He bent over, grabbing the cushions from the seat of the couch. When he had two of them stacked, he held them in front of his stomach and stood in front of Flash. "Go."

"Seriously?" Was the man actually giving Flash permission to punch him?

Pete smiled. Not a big thing, but it was there. "Afraid a cushion will bruise your tiny little—oof! Damn, man— you've got a hell of a kick," Pete wheezed out, stumbling back a step.

A minute passed with nothing but the muffled sounds of Flash punching light blue couch cushions and Pete grunting as he absorbed the blows.

"I told her we had to get married immediately, if not sooner, and she said no, and that's when you showed up." He finished this off with a quick three punches. "This is *supposed* to be my year to win it all. She was *supposed* to be a one-night stand. And we have to get married because I'm not going to let her keep that boy from me, even though it'll screw up all my plans. But she said *no.*"

Now that he'd hit something, he felt his anger going from a roiling boil to a low simmer. He punched the cushions one more time and sagged forward, his forehead resting on the top.

He had a son. The enormity of that fact still made him see stars. A healthy little boy who Brooke obviously loved and…

And she hadn't told him.

"Better?" Pete asked, sounding winded.

Flash nodded. He was breathing hard and his hands hurt, but the throbbing pain was good, anchoring him to his body.

Pete shifted, one arm coming up and lying over top of Flash's shoulder. Not that Flash needed a hug and not that this was a hug—but there was something comforting about it, all the same. "I guess I'm not as calm as I thought I was," he mumbled into the cushions.

"Did you hit anyone?" Pete asked, patting Flash on the back.

"Do you count?"

"Not today."

Flash shook his head. "Walked away when I needed to. Called you guys for backup when I realized I couldn't handle this myself."

"Didn't punch me in the face, either. All things considered, you're doing real well."

Flash snorted. It didn't feel like he was doing anything but losing it.

"You said you told her you were getting married?"

"Yeah." The thought left him uneasy. Marriage was... forever. Lawrence men—and Pete by extension—were one and done. If Flash married Brooke, that was it. He was *done*.

He'd do it. He'd do it in a heartbeat because that's what a father did for his son and, honestly, the sex was great. People throughout time had gotten married for less.

But...*marriage*.

To a woman who had no problem keeping secrets from him.

It was a recipe for disaster. And that was if she agreed. Huge *if*.

Pete was silent long enough that Flash lifted his head. When he'd been a hotheaded kid, he'd looked up to Pete

Wellington. The older man was a hell of a good rodeo rider, one Flash had aspired to be like. But for ten years, they'd been on opposite sides of a feud about the ownership of the All-Stars Rodeo. They'd made their peace, mostly, but it was still hard to think of this man as a friend.

Even if Flash suspected that's what Pete was. Who else would take a cushioned pummeling for Flash?

And now Pete was staring at Flash with a look of incredulous amusement on his face. "Where's the charm, Lawrence? I thought—*ow*—you were this legendary ladies' man. You could talk your way into any woman's bed and—*ugh*—make her feel like she was the only woman in the world."

"I am," Flash said, throwing another punch. He was going to owe Brooke a new couch, probably. "I was," he corrected.

He hadn't been that man since, well, since Brooke.

Maybe it wouldn't be so bad, a traitorous voice whispered in the back of his head. Great sex, yeah—but Brooke had gotten under his skin well before infants had come into play. Hell, he'd never looked up a one-night stand before, much less a year later. It might even be good...

But he'd have to trust her for that to happen, and she'd have to believe he wasn't the same asshole he'd been before he cleaned up his act, and, yeah, that felt like an impossible mountain to climb.

"You told her," Pete said yet again. "You *told* that woman to marry you, you giant jackass."

"Do you have a point?" Flash punctuated this with another combo punch. "Or are you just going to repeat yourself until the end of time?"

"What did you think would happen, issuing orders like that—to Brooke Bonner, of all people?" Flash paused mid-swing to stare at Pete, who rolled his eyes. "Next time, try *asking* her." Then he shoved Flash with the cushions.

Stumbling back, Flash gaped at Pete, who shook his head tauntingly.

Ask her?

Ask her to marry him. Like, down on one knee, with a ring and a promise.

Not an order. A proposal.

Like he cared about her.

Oh, hell—what had Flash done?

Eight

"I'm so sorry about this," Brooke said, leading Chloe Lawrence upstairs into the nursery, where Bean was screaming.

She felt like screaming, too. The nerve of that man, demanding that she rearrange her entire life—again—to get *married*.

Married! She had a comeback to orchestrate, a record to release, a tour to get through and a baby to announce to the world. Not to mention the whole mom thing, which was a full-time job all by itself. Who the hell had time for a wedding? Maybe in a few years…

Besides—Flash wasn't exactly making his case.

Yes, the sex was as amazing as ever, but she was not going to permanently tie herself to any man, much less one with an arrest record and a penchant for issuing orders. She had enough people in her life telling her what to do and when to do it, treating her as if she couldn't possibly make her own decisions about her life and her career. And now she had to deal with his sister because, of course, Flash had called in reinforcements to try and wear her down, no doubt.

She was more than tempted to call Alex for backup, but

that would undoubtedly lead to a brawl. And calling Crissy Bonner was out of the question—that'd be a brawl *and* a police report. For a brief second, Brooke debated calling Kyle Morgan, but that wouldn't work either, because Kyle would be just as stunned to find out about Bean as Flash had been.

No, Brooke was on her own here.

Then Chloe said, "Do not apologize for anything involving my brother," in a way that made it seem like she might consider Flash to be a butthead or something. When Brooke gave her a funny look, Chloe merely shrugged. "Look, I know he's got it bad for you and I also know I don't currently have all the facts, but just because he *wants* you doesn't mean he *deserves* you."

Brooke gaped at the woman in surprise because that was the thing she'd needed to hear right then. The second part, anyway.

What did she mean, Flash had it bad for Brooke?

"Thank you."

But Chloe wasn't listening. Instead, she'd moved to stand next to the crib, staring down at Bean with absolute adoration in her eyes. "Oh my. Oh, my *goodness*," she whispered, clutching her hands to her chest. "Look at you, sweetie. Hi, honey—I'm your aunt Chloe."

Brooke stepped around Chloe and picked Bean up. Chloe gasped, "Oh, he's *perfect*," her eyes filling with tears. "What's his name?"

"James Frasier Bonner, but I call him Bean," Brooke said.

"Can I hold him?" Chloe was already reaching out for the baby, but she stopped before actually plucking Bean from Brooke's arms. "I'm sorry. I'm just—this is such a surprise and I love babies so much and it's Flash's baby. You even gave him Flash's name!" She gave Brooke a watery smile.

"Sure. Here, take the rocker and we'll see if Bean is feeling sociable."

"Do you want to tell me what's happened?" Chloe said. "I gather that Flash didn't know about that little angel before a few hours ago?"

"No, he didn't. No one knows, really." She nestled Bean in Chloe's arms.

"Oh, goodness," the other woman whispered as Bean stared up at her. Then he turned on his father's charm and smiled at his aunt, who promptly began crying. That startled Bean and made him cry. Frankly, Brooke had no hope of holding herself together. It'd been *such* a long night.

"I'm so sorry," Chloe said again as Brooke took Bean back. "We've been trying to have a baby and…"

"It's okay." Brooke snatched the tissues and everyone took a moment to calm down. She felt terrible for Chloe—Brooke couldn't imagine dealing with infertility and then discovering a sibling had accidentally had a child despite taking precautions? Brooke couldn't fight the guilt that swamped her.

"I'm fine," Chloe said, and her gaze shifted to Brooke. "So how did my brother stick his foot into it this time?"

The story spilled out of Brooke. She tried to keep to just the facts, but then Chloe would say something like "Those headlines must have *horrified* you," or "He did *what*?" It probably wasn't smart to pour her heart out to this woman she barely knew and only in a professional capacity because Brooke had no idea what might be splashed across the internet tomorrow, but, God, it felt so good to talk to someone besides her mother and Alex. The isolation of the last few months caught up with her all at once, and, before she knew it, she was crying into a tissue and Chloe was rocking the baby and everything was still a huge mess. Amazingly, Brooke felt better.

As Brooke finished the story, Chloe gazed down on

Bean, who was playing with an expensive-looking neck-lace, his eyes drowsy. If Brooke was lucky, Chloe would be able to get the baby back to sleep, and if she was very lucky, no one would shout or slam a door or anything.

Brooke wasn't feeling that lucky.

"So let me see if I've got this right," Chloe said gently. "He told you that you had to marry him? He didn't even *ask*?"

"No!" Brooke said as quietly as she could. Thank God, Chloe got it. "And that's when you walked in."

"Such a jackass. Whoops, sorry, sweetie," she cooed to Bean, who blinked up at her and then launched an-other charming smile at his aunt. "But he didn't lose his temper?"

"I guess not?" Brooke swallowed. "I mean, he's got a right to be upset. But it was nothing like what those head-lines described."

Chloe smirked. "Did he tell you what the fight was about?"

"No?" That didn't sound good.

But Chloe didn't see fit to expand on that comment. In-stead, she looked at Brooke. A shiver went down Brooke's back because there was a calculating gleam in the woman's eyes that hadn't been there a moment ago.

"Here's the thing, though—he's not wrong." Brooke in-haled sharply as Chloe went on, "From a public relations point of view, I mean. If you two are married, we could spin this as a secret long-distance relationship instead of a wayward one-night stand. We could make it sound highly romantic while we release little teases of this supposed re-lationship without revealing too much, while we build up to exclusive interviews and magazine covers. We'd have both your audience and ours *hooked*. The press would be fantastic."

A pit of disquiet began to yawn open in Brooke's stomach. That was probably exactly what the record company would tell her to do, but…

Yes, she wanted to go public with her son. Yes, it made sense to have a plan. And the PR would probably be great.

But was it asking too much for it to be on her terms?

To try to keep some part of her private life private?

"I don't know if I like the sound of that," she told Chloe, trying to be diplomatic about it.

"It's a shame we can't retroactively get last year's date on the wedding certificate," Chloe mused, all of her attention on the baby. Brooke wasn't even sure Chloe had heard her. "But a lie you can prove wrong with a simple records search is a bad lie. Always lie as close to the truth as possible."

Brooke definitely did not like the sound of that. "I don't want to lie anymore."

"Not lie," Chloe went on. "We just want to bend the truth a little. You guys met, had an instant connection, but you couldn't get your schedules lined up…hmm. No, that won't work—Flash was kicked off the rodeo for half the season last year. He could have followed you around easily. No, you were hot and heavy until his arrest, and then you gave him an ultimatum to shape up, which he did."

"Can we slow down for a second here?" Brooke asked, because this was exactly what she was afraid of—Chloe was still going to strong-arm Brooke into doing what Flash wanted, just like Flash had tried to do. The only difference was that Chloe would do it while being all sympathetic and understanding instead of yelling. "There's no way my mother would approve of someone like Flash."

But there was no slowing Chloe. "So he straightened up and you guys have been secretly dating for…five months seems about right. And now that he's passed your tests with flying colors, you guys decided to get married! Yes, I like this. Flash gets his redemption story and you get a huge PR boost for your new album and—"

"I am *not* getting married right now," Brooke burst out.

"I understand your reluctance," Chloe said, not quite as sympathetic as she'd been before. "Flash has that effect on people. But here's the problem—beyond a redemption story or a marketing blitz, what if something happens to you, God forbid?" Before Brooke could panic at this statement—was this a *threat*?—Chloe went on. "Without the legal protection of marriage, would Flash be able to take custody of his own son? Or would your mother keep this perfect little angel away from his own father? Not that we wouldn't fight it in court," Chloe went on, smiling at Bean. "After all, what's the point in being billionaires if you can't buy the best lawyers?"

Billionaires? Brooke inhaled sharply. This *was* a threat.

"But it'd be a long, messy legal battle, one where Flash might not get to see his own son for a long time. I don't know what kind of person your mother is, but if you're concerned about her choices now…" She let the words trail off, her implication clear.

A churning panic took hold of Brooke's stomach because she was not going to get married so Flash could be redeemed and she was not going to marry anyone for the PR, but making sure Flash could care for his own son?

Because Chloe wasn't wrong.

Crissy Bonner might be disappointed that Brooke had gotten knocked up and she would definitely hate Flash, but she loved Bean. She loved being a grandmother and keeping Bean all to herself.

Brooke realized she didn't know how far Crissy would go to keep things that way—all while proclaiming it was *for the best*, no doubt.

"Is that a risk you're willing to take?" Chloe finished softly. "I wouldn't."

"I'm not on death's doorstep," Brooke said, surprised to hear her voice shake. She surged to her feet and plucked

Bean out of Chloe's arms. "I don't have to marry your brother to make sure he gets to see his child, and if you're only here to be the good cop to Flash's bad cop, then you can leave. *Now.*"

She didn't wait for an answer as she stormed from the room and headed downstairs. She was done talking, done with the entire Lawrence family. God, she felt like a fool. Nothing had changed. She and Flash were electric together, but sexual chemistry only got a girl so far. She was not going to let a little lust blind her to the big picture.

She got to the bottom of the stairs and glanced at the front door. Had it only been—what, an hour since Flash had pressed her back against the door and made her feel exactly like the girl she used to be?

Less than an hour. Less than an evening for Flash Lawrence to blow into her life like a twister, leaving a wake of destruction in his path.

And who had to clean up after the storm had passed? She did. Again.

Starting right now, she and Flash were on a no-touching basis. She couldn't afford to be selfish anymore. She had to be a mother, and if that meant it was her against Flash, the Lawrence family, her own family, her record label and, hell, the whole world, then that's the battle Brooke would fight.

She was done hiding and done apologizing. As much as she might miss the girl she'd been before, she was a different woman now. There was no going back.

She strode into the library, her mouth open to tell everyone to get the hell out—but what she saw made her stumble to a stop. Flash had Pete Wellington pinned against the far wall and was punching him in the stomach again and again as Pete grunted in pain, like something out of her nightmares.

"What are you doing?" she cried out in horror.

Nine

Flash spun midpunch, stumbled and almost lost his balance. "Brooke?"

Bean began to cry and Pete said, "Oh, hell."

Damn it.

"It's not what it looks like," he said in what he hoped was a calm voice. He'd just figured out how he'd screwed up. He couldn't afford to make this worse.

"He's not hurting me," Pete called over his shoulder, although the slightly pained tone of his voice made it seem like a lie.

"That's not what it looks like?" Brooke edged toward the door, tucking the baby so Flash couldn't even see the kid.

Oh, God—if she ran now, he had no idea when he'd get to see his son again, and that was a risk he wasn't willing to take. So he said, "It's not. I'm hitting cushions."

"Cushions?" Brooke's eyes bugged out of her head.

"It's okay. No one's in any danger," he said.

It hurt, the look in her eyes. She was furious and scared and exhausted, and Flash wasn't making anything better. God, he never should've ordered her to marry him. Pete had been exactly right. Obviously Brooke felt backed into a corner.

"What's wrong?" Chloe said, running into the room. "Who's hurt?"

"No one," Flash said as calmly as he could—which, all things considered, actually did come out calmly. He owed one to Pete for helping him get to this point because if the man hadn't had the idea to punch a couch, Flash knew he wouldn't be able to think, much less act rationally.

What a mess.

"Brooke? I was hitting cushions."

"Cushions," Pete confirmed. He stepped around Flash, holding the cushions up. "From the couch. See?"

"It's okay," Chloe said softly, reaching out to pat Bean, who was not having a great night, either. None of them were.

"Why would you do that?" Brooke said, looking completely bewildered.

Aw, hell. He'd never wanted a do-over so badly in his entire life. He'd hit the chute at the start of the ride but, unlike in the rodeo, he wasn't going to get a reride. The night had started so well, but then she'd dropped the bomb about the baby, and since then he had not handled things well. He needed to get back to where she was in his arms and he remembered how to be the charming guy she wanted and they weren't on opposite sides.

"Like primal scream therapy, you know? Just blowing off steam so I could think. It was a controlled release. It's okay," he repeated.

"Don't you dare try that—*charm*, Flash Lawrence," Brooke said, her voice cracking as she backed away from Chloe's touch. "Nothing about this is okay!"

"I know," Flash said through gritted teeth, holding his hands out in the sign of surrender. He kept plenty of distance between him and Brooke and shot a look at Chloe that said, *Back off.* Which, to her credit, she did. Crowding Brooke right now would only make the fight-or-flight reaction worse.

"It'll be okay." He lied because he didn't trust her, she clearly didn't trust him, and neither of those facts changed reality—in this case, the baby boy who was making pitifully sad noises.

Brooke looked from worried face to worried face. Chloe helped Pete put the cushions back on the couch, leaving the exit open. Brooke eyed them warily, but she didn't bolt, and for that Flash was thankful.

"You weren't attacking him," she said, dropping her gaze as her cheeks shot scarlet.

Flash had the overwhelming urge to sweep her into his arms, take her upstairs and tuck her in. Then, in the morning, they'd have a good laugh about this. Ha-ha-ha.

"No."

"He really wasn't," Pete added, thankfully no longer sounding winded. Flash glanced back to see Chloe and Pete standing side by side, his arm around her shoulders as she leaned into him, her gaze fastened on Brooke and the baby. Flash got the feeling that Pete was holding Chloe back. He caught Flash's gaze and nodded encouragingly. "Miss Bonner, I know you don't know me from Adam, but I've known Flash for almost eleven years now and I'd swear on a Bible in a court of law that he's not the same immature, hotheaded jerk he used to be."

"Thanks, Pete, but I got it from here," Flash grumbled.

"It was my idea for him to hit the cushions," Pete went on. "I was just holding them."

"Oh, my God, I'm such a fool," Brooke blurted out, shifting Bean so she could swipe the back of her hand over her eyes.

More than her hard *no* to his terrible proposal, more than the surprise of the baby, it was the sight of Brooke

trying not to cry that did him in. He was so mad at her—
that wasn't going away. But he also wanted to take care
of her and those two things weren't playing nicely inside
his head.

"No, you're not," Flash said quickly. "Nothing tonight
has been normal." There had to be a way to fix this, damn
it. But how? Well, an apology was a good place to start.
"I'm sorry, babe."

She made a noise that was halfway between a sob and
a laugh. "Do you even know what you're apologizing for
this time, or are you just guessing again?"

"It's a long list," he agreed, managing to put a good smile
into it. "But top of the list is that I shouldn't have told you
we had to get married. Even if it's a good idea."

"No," Brooke said, her voice shaky and her eyes huge,
"you shouldn't have. No one should've." She cut a glance
at Chloe. Flash didn't follow Brooke's gaze, but he heard
Chloe sigh. "I don't want to be forced into anything."

That Flash understood completely. He'd always been
the kind of guy who'd get a direct order and do the exact
opposite just to prove he could. God, why hadn't he seen
her reaction coming? He'd just been so convinced of the
rightness of him and Brooke being together that he'd stam-
peded right over her.

Brooke sniffed again, dashing more tears off her cheeks.
Flash wanted to fold Brooke into his arms and make everything okay again. But it was clear that doing anything like
that would just make Brooke dig in her heels even deeper.
Sometimes, a man had to call a tactical retreat if he wanted
to live to fight another day.

Figuratively speaking, of course.

"It's been a long night and you've got to be exhausted
from the show," he said, trying to give her a nice smile.
"I'm truly sorry how this evening has gone down. I think
it's time for us to leave so you and James can get some

sleep." And he could figure out what Chloe had said that had thrown Brooke into such a panic.

He wanted her. He didn't trust her. He needed to marry her.

God, what a freaking *mess*.

Brooke stared down at the baby. Even Flash could tell the boy was uncomfortable, squirming in his mother's arms. "We can try, anyway."

He came damn close to offering to stay the night so she could sleep and he could rock his son in his arms and get to know the boy. And then he'd be here in the morning when Brooke woke up and they could...

Well, the odds of them having great sex again seemed so small right now as to be nonexistent. But they could talk, hopefully without panic or bitterness.

But discretion was the better part of valor, damn it. And he needed to regroup in a serious way. So, instead, he said, "I'd like to see you again so we can try this whole talking thing. I'm in town through..." He thought quickly. He didn't have to be in Lexington, Kentucky, for ten days, which didn't seem like enough time to get this situation resolved peacefully.

Crud. His lead in the rankings was tenuous. Skipping a rodeo would knock him down several places and might ultimately cost him the Cowboy of the Year championship.

But then he looked at Brooke again and sighed. Missing one rodeo wouldn't be the end of the world. Just so long as it didn't become a habit. Surely, in a week or two they could get some sort of custody plan or visitation schedule set up, and he could come right back to Nashville after the rodeo.

"For as long as you need me to be," he corrected. "We can meet here or in public, wherever you want. Bring Alex."

He didn't want Alex there because Alex would probably beat the ever-loving hell out of him, and Flash would have no choice but to take it.

"You're being charming again," she mumbled, but he caught the way she tucked her lower lip under her teeth and peeked at him.

"Trying to," he agreed with an easy smile. That little flash of normalcy was encouraging. If everything could just calm down, he was sure he could talk sense into Brooke. He truly did want what was best for her and for their son. Brooke in his life was what he wanted. And if that included her being in his bed, well that was just icing on the cake.

"Flash, we need to have a plan—" Chloe started to say.

Flash held up a hand, cutting her off. "Nothing needs to be decided tonight. The only thing that needs to happen right now is Brooke needs to take care of herself and the baby. That's it." And he needed to get a grip on his priorities.

The look Brooke shot him was full of worry and hope and maybe just a little appreciation. At least, he hoped it was appreciation. "I have a meeting at one tomorrow to discuss the Bluebird show. I suppose we could meet after that? Maybe for coffee?" She glanced back at Chloe and Pete again. "Just the two of us. No offense."

It was Pete who answered. "None taken."

Flash worked real hard not to show his disappointment. Because he *wasn't* disappointed that she wasn't asking him to stay. He was happy that she wasn't insisting they bring their seconds to the meeting. Really, it was great news that Brooke was still willing to talk to him at all. "You name the place and I'll be there. Just text me."

She nodded and then looked toward the door. Right. They were leaving—now.

Chloe and Pete got the hint. They stepped forward, Chloe's gaze locked on to the baby. "My deepest apologies for coming on too strong," Chloe said, regret filling her voice. She reached out and, when Brooke didn't shy away, Chloe rubbed James's back. "I hope we can see this special little guy again soon?"

"I'll set it up with Flash." Brooke didn't sound too sure about it, though.

"Thank you," Chloe said, her voice cracking. "He's such a beautiful baby."

Pete held her tight and said, "Miss Bonner, we love your music. Can't wait for the new stuff. And no matter what, welcome to the family." Then he led his wife away.

As the front door opened, Flash heard Chloe almost whimper, "Oh Pete—that baby!"

"I know, hon. I know," Pete replied, his voice choked with emotion.

Then they were gone and Flash was alone with Brooke. "I'm sorry about that. I thought they were going to help," he said quietly.

"Did they?" She didn't move back, didn't shield the baby with her body.

"Pete did. This was—*is* a lot. For both of us." He closed the distance between them and lifted James out of her arms. Thank goodness she didn't resist. He tucked the baby under his chin. This, at least, he was pretty good at. He'd had plenty of practice holding Trixie, after all. He should probably thank Oliver for that—right after Oliver got done tearing him a new one for getting Brooke pregnant in the first place.

Man, this was one of the bigger messes he'd ever been in.

"I don't think I've ever apologized *for* my sister before," he went on. "Usually it's the other way around."

Brooke looked at him, her eyes huge and tired. But despite the toll the night had taken on her—on them all— Flash was pretty damn sure he'd never seen anyone as beautiful as she was. "It's fine, Flash," she said. He couldn't tell if she was being honest or not. "I suspect that you Lawrences are a hardheaded lot."

"Guilty as charged," he said with a good-natured grin. He patted James's back. "Thank you for this—for *him*. I don't know if I said that earlier or not."

"No, you didn't." Her face softened as she looked at the two of them. Wildly, Flash hoped she liked what she saw. Because he wasn't going to give this kid up. Hell, no. Whether she married him or not, whether he forgave her or not, they were in this together.

It'd be so much easier if they were really together, though. There had to be a way.

Flash pressed a tender kiss to the top of James's head. "Sleep for your mom, okay, sweetie?" Then he turned his attention back to Brooke. "Is there anything else I can do for you tonight?"

He knew she wasn't going to ask him to stay, not after he'd made a royal ass of himself tonight. But that didn't change things.

Damn it. He needed to marry her to make things legal for the baby. But did he seriously want to marry her?

He'd dreamed of this woman for a year. He thought he'd been dreaming of the sex, the easy jokes. What if he'd really been dreaming of something more?

Something more had to wait.

He had to man up and make things right. Any potential feelings he had for Brooke would come later, if they came at all.

"I'll… I'll see you tomorrow?" she said softly, taking a sleepy James back from Flash. Then her gaze dropped to his lips.

This wasn't Flash's first rodeo. "Tomorrow," he agreed, his voice barely a whisper. Then he leaned forward and brushed his lips against hers.

He didn't linger, didn't press the issue. "Call me for any reason. I can be right back out here in under twenty minutes." He'd have to see about getting a different hotel room closer to her house.

She nodded, looking breathless. Flash was sorely tempted to lean in for another kiss, something longer and hotter and…

Yeah, no. He backed away before he let his dick do the thinking. That's what had gotten them into this mess in the first place. "Good night, Brooke."

He was almost out of the room when she spoke. "Flash?"

Yes. But he didn't cheer. He turned and asked, "What, babe?"

"This can't get out yet. I can't have my mother finding out about you. Not…" Even across the room in the dark, he saw her swallow nervously. "Not yet."

Hadn't she mentioned her mother earlier? Brooke's record company and mother had all decided that she had to keep her pregnancy and baby a secret because Brooke wouldn't name him as the father? And now Brooke wasn't necessarily afraid of the press finding out about the baby, but she was clearly worried about her mother.

That bothered him. Damn it. He wished his own mother was still here. She'd be able to tell Flash if that was a normal mother-daughter thing or not. But maybe his sister-in-law Renee could shine a little light on how tense mother-daughter relationships worked. He'd have to ask, after Oliver got done chewing him out.

"I won't. No one outside of Chloe and Pete will know until you're ready to tell them. Well," he quickly corrected, "Chloe and Pete and my older brother, Oliver, and his wife, who's Chloe's best friend. It doesn't go farther than that."

They'd all wait to tell Milt Lawrence for a little bit. If Dad found out he had another grandbaby, life would get very complicated very fast.

"Your brother and his wife? Will they keep it quiet?"

"Absolutely. But outside of them, no one will know. You can hold me to that, Brooke."

She sagged in what he hoped was relief. "Okay. Good. Um, good night."

"Night, babe." Then, moving as quickly as he could, he walked his butt right out of that house and started thinking hard about tomorrow.

How did a man propose a marriage of convenience the second time after completely botching the first time?

Ten

"So you'll think about it?" Kari Stockard said, trailing after Brooke as she walked out of the conference room. "The press we'd get from the baby pictures alone could put your album sales over the top, Brooke. You know that."

"Yes, you said as much in the meeting." Repeatedly. Kari was a fine PR manager, but Brooke could take only so much browbeating, and what should've been a quick check-in about the Bluebird performance had instead been Brooke on one side of a conference table and seven—seven!—executives, managers and other people wearing suits on the other side, all trying to tell her what to do with her personal life. And they didn't even know about Flash yet.

Brooke had done a thorough internet check before she'd walked into that meeting this morning, and there was nothing connecting her and Flash. Bless Kyle Morgan's heart, he'd kept his mouth shut.

Brooke wished she'd brought Alex as backup today—but this was supposed to have been a short meeting, not the full-court press, so she'd told her best friend to take the day off because she wasn't up to the conversation Alex would want to have about Flash. Brooke hadn't even brought Mom, who was technically her manager. Instead, Mom was at home with Bean. Not that Mom would've been much help, anyway. She would've agreed to everything the label wanted, as evidenced by her parting shot this morning, which had been, "Sweetheart, don't you think that, with the album release coming up, you're going to want to tell the world about Jimmy?" No one called Bean that except for Crissy Bonner.

"The timing is perfect," Kari went on, still trailing Brooke. "Think of the buzz!"

So, yeah, Brooke was on her own here and it was exhausting. Was it wrong to want someone in her court? She picked up the pace. If she could make it to her car…well, then she could go meet with Flash and fight a completely different battle.

She didn't want it to be a battle, though. She wanted… to feel like she was in control of something. Anything.

Kari wasn't giving up anytime soon. She matched Brooke's pace. "We wouldn't even have to name the father. We could say you'd done in vitro! From a sperm bank?"

"Nope." She was practically jogging at this point. "When I'm ready to take him public, I'll let you know." She made the door.

"Before the album drops?" Kari yelled after her.

"You, too!" Brooke called over her shoulder, intentionally mishearing Kari's question. Her head hurt. Kari didn't know who Flash was so there'd been no discussion of a redemption arc or marriage, but, otherwise, Kari's plan was practically identical to what Chloe had outlined last night.

Brooke got to her car and paused long enough to make sure Kari hadn't trailed her before she slumped back in the seat. The day of public reckoning was coming, that much was certain. But would it involve a wedding or just a baby?

She just wanted to write her songs and perform, and,

yeah, she wanted to make a lot of money—money she controlled, not her mother or her uncle, the rat bastard. Being raised by a single mother meant that Brooke hadn't grown up rich. But everything else that went with being famous? It was all a huge pain in the ass, frankly.

She sat for a moment, trying to get her thoughts in order. Which, of course, took the shape of a melody. Somewhere in the middle of the night, dozing in the chair with Bean, the song in her head had shifted to something darker, something more raw. *Don't say something romantic* was still there, but another song was lurking at the edge of her subconscious.

The stripped-down acoustics of the new melody ran through her mind, full of anguish. A song about being stuck in an impossible situation with no right answers. She opened the notes program on her phone and dictated the lyrics. If nothing else, art imitating her life made for good inspiration.

God, this was a mess.

Because the fact was that everything Chloe Lawrence had said last night hadn't been wrong. Legally, Flash was a persona non grata when it came to Bean. He wasn't on the birth certificate and, until paternity tests happened, he couldn't prove that he was Bean's father, although all anyone had to do was look at the way those two smiled to see the truth.

It didn't matter how Chloe or Kari promised to spin it to her advantage—the simple truth was that for a few weeks, the press would be brutal. All the more so because she'd had the nerve to hide her pregnancy and child this long. Maybe it was selfish or cowardly, but she didn't want to face it alone.

Part of hitting it big last year had been the public perception that Brooke Bonner didn't screw around, do drugs or drink. She might write some saucy songs, but she was a role model to girls—play by the rules and you'll go far. Shattering that mostly true image with an out-of-wedlock baby would cost her fans.

Getting married to Flash—and quickly—meant that she wouldn't have to face the press on her own. It'd also mean she wouldn't have to hide the fact that she was sleeping with him. Assuming she was going to keep sleeping with him.

Was she assuming that?

Just thinking about the orgasm last night kicked her pulse up a notch. But that perfect moment, like the one in Fort Worth over a year ago, was completely overshadowed by what came afterward.

How was marrying Flash the smart thing to do?

The words *but how could I say no?* popped into her mind. Frankly, after that meeting, Brooke could use a drink. *I could use a shot of something stronger,* she dictated, letting the words flow, feeling her way toward what came next.

Can't afford the mistake the whiskey would help me make?

Yeah, it needed work. And she was stalling. She'd told Mom she had a coffee date planned with Kyle Morgan to go over a song. And she was, technically, thinking about lyrics, so it wasn't a total lie. But she had an afternoon to decide the direction of her life for the immediate future before everything spun out of control for her again.

She knew what she had to do. She needed to ask Flash to meet her at a coffee shop. Where are you? she texted.

He answered back in seconds. My hotel. Where do you want to meet? Clearly, he'd been waiting on her. The thought made her relax just a bit.

The responsible thing to do would be to name a bar or restaurant or coffee shop. They needed to stay in public, as part of a crowd, so they could have a mature, rational discussion about parenting and not getting married like adults. That certainly would be the smart course of action.

But all the logic in the world didn't seem to apply when it came to her and Flash. She wanted to feel like she had a choice. And, damn it all, she wanted him. In a bed, this time. Yeah, she was apparently going to keep sleeping with him. *What's your room number?*

The replay came immediately: *623—you want to meet here?*

She wanted a do-over of last night, before it'd all blown up in her face. Just him and her and no big surprises, waiting to ruin everything, lurking in the wings this time. Brooke wanted more than fifteen minutes of satisfaction in Flash's arms. It was selfish, sure. And after last night, it was clearly a mistake of epic proportions.

But, apparently, when it came to Flash, she'd just willfully keep making that mistake.

I'm still not marrying you, she typed, hitting the letters with extra force. *Just FYI.*

Noted, he replied.

It was so hard to tell if he was looking forward to her showing up or if he was bracing himself for the worst or what. Well, he could just brace. She needed a little more from him. Just for her. Then they could go back to being co-parents or whatever.

I'm coming to you, she texted, and then started the car.

Just as she pulled out of the parking lot, he texted back, *Thank God.*

Brooke knocked on the door, at least 73 percent sure she was making a mistake. But before she could bail, it swung open and Flash was there.

Damn, he made rugged look *so* good.

He wore a black All-Stars T-shirt, which showed off his muscled forearms. But the funny thing was his feet were bare. No boots, no socks. He gave her that look that she'd always been powerless to resist. "Hey, come in. Thanks for making it."

"No problem."

A memory pushed to the forefront of her mind, of the last time she'd been alone in a hotel room with this man. Of Flash pressing her against the door and whispering in her ear, "Tell me what you want," as he'd ground his erection against her, her entire body humming with need for him. "I'm going to give it to you, Brooke," he'd all but growled in her ear. "But be honest."

She shuddered and shoved the memory away. Now was *so* not the time for erotic flashbacks. God, meeting in his room really was an awful idea, wasn't it? She hadn't even been alone with him for thirty seconds and she was already thinking about sex.

Flash shut the door behind her and, dang it, she startled. He had a knowing smirk on his face. "You sure you want to meet here?"

"No." She didn't like this awkwardness between them and she liked it even less that she was the only one feeling it.

Once upon a time, she had promised him honesty. She'd done a terrible job of that when it came to Bean. Being upfront with Flash now was the very least she could do for him. So she took a deep breath and said, "I don't think I should be alone with you."

He chuckled, not looking the least insulted. God, Brooke just wanted to curl into him but, no, she couldn't. She had to remember why she was here and, more importantly, how she'd gotten to this point. Neither of them would be in this position if she and Flash had been able to keep their hands to themselves.

"If you're not supposed to be alone with me," he asked slowly, "what are you doing here?"

"If we met in public, we'd run the risk of being spotted." It wasn't a great excuse.

And Flash knew it. His gaze sharpened. "Are you saying you've decided to keep *this*," he said, motioning between them, "a secret?"

"No. I'm saying I don't want public perception to force our hand." She turned away from him because it was hard to think with him like that. He looked so damn good in this hotel room.

Wow, she hadn't realized he had a corner suite instead of a regular room. This place was bigger—and nicer—than the apartment she and her mom had shared for most of her adolescence. She certainly hadn't been able to afford rooms this nice when she'd been touring—especially not after her uncle embezzled all her earnings.

This was a *very* nice room. Huge windows behind a dining room table set for eight showed her the view of Music Row and the Cumberland River. She was standing in a living room that not only had a couch and matching accent chairs and tasteful lamps—not industrial light fixtures, but real lamps with stylish shades—but the whole thing was arranged on top of an expensive-looking Persian rug. An office area backed up to a full wet bar. Next to the dining room table, to the left, there was what looked like a full kitchen and a set of doors to the right where, she assumed, there was a bathroom and a bedroom. With a bed. Probably a nice one.

Nope. Not thinking about the bed Flash slept in.

She turned her back on those doorways and walked toward the window overlooking Music Row. Even though this was probably one of the nicer hotel rooms she'd ever been in, she could still tell that Flash had settled in. Behind one of the accent chairs was a duffel bag with a protective vest and ropes spilling out—his bull ropes, no doubt. Chaps were draped over one of the dining room chairs and his black hat was tossed onto the granite countertop. Coffee cups were scattered around the coffeepot on the wet bar, along with a few plastic grocery bags.

Okay, so Flash wasn't the neatest of guys. Somehow, that made him seem more…real. More normal, anyway. He wasn't just this perfect fantasy she'd created or this thug the headlines had painted him to be. He was a flesh-and-blood man.

One who could afford the best room in the hotel, apparently. Rodeo riders weren't known for their tastes for the finer things in life. Half of them lived out of their cars during the summer or crashed on floors because the money from rodeos was only good if one was winning. Hadn't Chloe said something about the Lawrence family being billionaires? It'd been couched in a vaguely threatening statement about affording the best lawyers, but…

Was Flash actually rich?

"I got you some tea," he said, startling her out of her thoughts. "I didn't know which kind, so there's a few sample packs. The concierge found an electric kettle so you wouldn't have coffee-flavored tea to drink."

Oh no—thoughtfulness. This was terrible—if Flash was going to be both charming *and* thoughtful, she was doomed. "Any green tea?"

"Jasmine or peach?" She heard the sound of him rustling through the bags. "Oh—there's a plain green in here, too."

"Jasmine, please." She couldn't let herself be sweet-talked. She had to remember why she was here, and it wasn't because she'd missed Flash or he'd missed her or even that they'd been great in bed together and would probably get even better.

She was here because Bean was almost four months old and had spent a whopping twenty minutes with his father. She was here to ensure that Flash was a man of his word and really had turned his life around. That everyone last night had been telling the truth when they'd said Flash was just hitting pillows and that his whole family and their possible billions of dollars wouldn't be used to cower her into submission. She was here to make sure her son would be safe with Flash.

That *she* was safe with Flash. She wanted to know that he wouldn't make her fall in love with him and then rip her heart right out of her chest. That he wouldn't force her into a marriage and then force her to choose between her child and her career. She needed to believe that he wouldn't abandon her to deal with the hard realities of parenthood alone while he chased the rodeo once the naked lust between them cooled.

Because it would cool, right?

Flash wasn't the kind of guy who settled down. He played the field, kept his options open and never met a woman he didn't love.

Except…was that him? He sure as hell had been that a year ago when she'd taken him up on everything he'd had to offer.

But he'd been waiting for her outside the Bluebird. He'd come to her house. He'd said repeatedly that he hadn't looked at another woman since their night together, and his sister had casually mentioned that she knew Flash had it bad for Brooke. Would he be faithful to her—even if they didn't get hitched? Was she even being fair to ask that of him if she kept telling him no?

The fact was that she wanted it all—great sex with a perfect man who made her feel wonderful *and* her career *and* an equal partner to raise Bean.

But she knew if she asked for that, he'd be hustling her down the aisle before she could do anything else and there'd be no guarantee she'd get anything on her wish list. No matter how much charm Flash wielded right now, he wouldn't be in a big hurry to drop the rodeo and be a stay-at-home dad. The rodeo was in his blood, just like the music was in hers.

She couldn't have it all. There simply weren't enough hours in the day. Which meant she couldn't have Flash. She had to put her son first. Her selfish wants and physical needs came last.

No, not last. Marketing plans and press releases and, *ugh*, magazine covers with exclusive interviews and redemption arcs and record sales—all of those things were dead last on her to-do list. But that didn't mean she could ignore them.

Lord, what a mess. She rubbed her eyes.

"Did you get some sleep?" he asked behind her. She could just make out his reflection in the glass window. He was leaning against the wet bar, watching her. "You look better."

So much for that legendary charm. She knew exactly what she looked like—cutoff shorts, a loose-fitting black tee and a Nashville Predators ball cap pulled over an extremely messy ponytail. She looked exactly like a woman who'd had a terrible night. "That's the best you've got?"

Flash came to stand beside her, grinning wildly. He traced his fingers over her shoulder and down her arm until he laced his fingers with hers. She shivered at the touch and fought the urge to rest her head on his shoulder. "I could say that I've never seen you look more beautiful than you do right now, but we're past flattery, don't you think?" Leaning closer, his voice dropped to a deep whisper. "Here's the thing, babe—I'm not going to lie to you. Never have and I'm not about to start."

She blushed because she realized he was right. He'd told her up front about his arrest record. She was the one who'd kept secrets. "Okay. Yes. I, uh, I apologize again for not telling you about the baby." When he didn't answer right away, she asked, "Are you still mad at me?"

He squeezed her hand—and took his sweet time answering. The longer he was silent, the more her stomach sank. How was this going to work?

Finally, he said, "I'm still working on it. I want to trust you but…" He went on before she could interrupt, "I get that you did the best you could with the information you had." He cleared his throat. "And I'm sorry I didn't handle last night well. I won't attempt to make decisions for you again."

This was the Flash who'd been waiting for her behind the Bluebird Cafe, the one who said all the right things at all the right times. This was the Flash who made her want him.

This was not the Flash who had to walk out of a room before he lost his temper or hit cushions to keep control. This wasn't the Flash who issued life-changing orders and just expected her to go along with them, no questions asked.

Which one was the real Flash Lawrence?

"Seriously, though—did you sleep?" The way he asked made it clear he really wanted to know. He wasn't just making polite small talk.

At least, she hoped he wasn't. "A few hours. No one sleeps well with a fussy four-month-old on their chest. Mom thinks he might be teething. Which is super early, but not unheard-of, apparently."

He winced. "That's going to suck. My niece is teething and it's rough for all of them. I don't want you to have to deal with that on your own."

How was she supposed to interpret that? She'd made it clear she wasn't marrying him—but was he implying that he'd be around to help share the load? Or he'd take Bean back to his place? Which was, presumably… Texas, maybe? Or did he mean he'd hire a nanny or something?

Before she could ask, the kettle beeped and he left her side to get the water. She absolutely wasn't going to miss his warmth, for heaven's sake. He was all of five feet away. It's not like she couldn't go five minutes without touching him. She'd managed a whole year without him!

But then he asked, "How much honey do you take with your tea?" and she knew she was in trouble because, seriously, this level of thoughtfulness was dangerous.

"You remembered I like honey?"

Flash paused midstride and then spun back to her, an almost predatory gleam in his eye. "Do you know," he said, his voice suddenly that much lower and that much deeper, and her traitorous body vibrated like a tuning fork at exactly the right pitch, "that every time I kiss you, I taste honey on your sweet lips?"

"No," she said breathlessly as he backed her against the window, his hard body making her soft with need.

"I do." His breath caressed her lips as his hands came to her hips, pulling her against him. The hot length of his erection pushed against her and she couldn't help the moan that escaped her. "I could get drunk on your kiss and never want for water again."

Oh. Oh, *my*.

"Good line," she whispered, tilting her head up for him.

"You can have it." But he didn't take the kiss she offered. He held himself back, which was probably a sign of maturity or something ridiculous like that. "Not gonna lie, Brooke—I want you so bad." He thrust against her and she moaned. He made a matching sound of need, and she couldn't think, couldn't do anything but feel him against her, want him inside her.

Then he cruelly pulled away. Not far, but enough that he wasn't pressing against her anymore. "Right now, we don't have to do anything except talk." His hand trailed up her side, over her ribs, skimming the edge of her breast before his fingers spread across her throat, and then he cupped her cheek in his palm, his thumb stroking over her skin. Her eyes fluttered closed and she let herself just *feel*.

No one else made her feel like Flash did.

"That's why you're here, isn't it?"

Was it? That's what she'd told herself last night, and then he'd given her an amazing orgasm against the door. She hadn't been able to think until they'd gotten the sex out of the way.

She could've met him in public today, could've insisted on a chaperone. She could've made him come back out to the house and subjected him to her mother, made him change Bean's diapers.

Instead, she'd come straight to his hotel room. He hadn't had to convince her of anything. She was here willingly.

She was *his* willingly.

"No," she whispered, lacing her fingers through his hair and pulling him down to her. "It's not."

Eleven

Hers. That's the word that crossed her mind when she crushed her lips against his.

This man was hers.

He always had been, since the very first moment he'd taken her hand and bowed over it like some lordly duke. If nothing else, they had this.

"Bed?" Flash asked against her mouth, his hands skimming down her back, over her bottom.

"Bed," she agreed.

She loved the hot, heavy sex against the door, but a window wasn't quite as reassuring. Besides, she wanted the luxury of limbs twining together, his bare skin against hers.

The next thing she knew, Flash had bent over and swept her legs out from underneath her. "Whoa!" she squeaked, throwing her arms around his neck for balance.

"I've got you, babe." Oh, she'd needed to hear that. "Do you have any idea what I want to do to you?"

She leaned forward and kissed the side of his neck. His pulse beat wildly against her lips. "Tell me."

"I want to feast on your body and make you scream my name when you come, and then I want to hold you afterwards until you've come back down to earth, and then I want to bury myself in your body until you break again, until I can't take it anymore. I want to lay you out and spend the next two days making love to you," he growled against her ear. Then he wrapped his lips around her lobe and tugged gently as he carried her back through the suite. "Then I want to do it again."

Every muscle in her body clenched at his charged words and, given the wolfish grin he shot her, she knew he'd felt it, too. She'd done that once with him, that glorious night in Fort Worth when he'd swept her off her feet.

Once a year wasn't enough.

Sadly, though, reality wasn't on their side. "We—oh, *Flash*," she moaned as he kissed her neck, "we don't have that kind of time." But Lord, it sounded wonderful, didn't it? A few days to explore how deep this connection went. A few days to selfishly enjoy this man and his tremendous skills.

Because the man had *skills*.

"Then I'll take the time I get with you." He kicked open the door to the bedroom and then kicked it shut, all without missing a single stride.

"Another good line," she murmured as he set her down on the bed and pulled her hat from her head.

"I'm full of them." Her hair tumbled wildly around her shoulders, the ponytail a distant memory. He paused, sucking in air. "God, Brooke—do you have any idea what you do to me?"

She leaned forward, stroking a hand over his obvious erection through his jeans. "I'm getting one."

"You…" He swallowed as she rested her head against his stomach and began to work the buttons on his fly loose.

She shoved his jeans down, then hooked her fingers into the waistband of his blue boxer briefs, which hugged his narrow hips, his ass, his *everything*. Then she pulled and he sprung free.

"If you don't want me to taste you, you let me know."

Flash groaned, his fingers finding her hair as her hands found his hot length. "Please," he got out through gritted teeth as she stroked him. "I want you to do what you want, Brooke," he moaned when she gave him a little squeeze. "I won't tell you what to do."

"You did last night."

There was something powerful about this moment. She had him in the palm of her hand—literally—and she could do what she wanted with him. She looked up at him through her eyelashes and then, slowly, pressed her lips to his tip. He shuddered, but before his hips could flex, she'd pulled away and ran the pad of her thumb over the area she'd kissed.

"A mistake. A huge one," he groaned, his head falling back. "You're killing me, babe."

"Don't mess up again," she said, knowing it sounded like an order. But it wasn't, not really. She was all but begging him.

She'd given him a second chance last night when he'd told her he'd sobered up and straightened himself out, only to have him struggle when she told him about Bean. Yeah, that was partly her fault because she'd broken the news in the absolute worst way possible. But she hadn't forgotten the hard edge to his voice when he'd informed her that they were getting married as soon as possible. And that didn't even take into account the awful moment when she'd thought he'd been attacking his brother-in-law.

She didn't need a domineering, immature jerk in her life. She needed a man, one who did right by her and her son, one who stood up for her, not to her.

She needed Flash to be that man.

"You get one more chance," she told him in all seriousness.

"I won't fail you again." His grip on her hair loosened and then was gone entirely as he tilted her head back. "You can count on me, Brooke—now and forever. No matter what we decide, we're in this together." Even through the haze of lust, she could see how serious he was.

"I know," she whispered, emotion clogging up her throat.

He leaned down and kissed her, the kind of kiss that said as much as his words had. It wasn't a kiss of frenzied passion, but one of heat and something richer, deeper.

Something that might even be love.

No, no—she wasn't going to let love get hopelessly mixed up with lust. Especially not right now. This time with him right now—this was about satisfaction and then about planning. Neither of those two things had a damn thing to do with love.

They'd had so little time together that she hardly knew what this man looked like nude. One night together and a few stolen moments—plus several hard, awkward conversations.

"Take these all the way off," she demanded, releasing her grip on him. "I want you naked."

"God, yes." He stumbled back, kicking out of his pants and yanking his shirt over his head. "I'll always give you what you want. You know that, right?"

She nodded as she did away with what was left of her ponytail and started to pull her shirt off. Flash stopped her. "Just be honest with me, Brooke. Not just about sex—about everything. Be honest with yourself."

Then he grabbed the hem of her shirt and lifted it over her head. She'd gone with the pretty teal bra today, one of the only non-nursing bras she owned that still fit. Her boobs looked *huge* in it.

"Okay to touch?" he asked, stroking a finger down her chest.

She started to nod but then stopped. Last night had been

about reclaiming a part of the girl she'd been before she'd become a mother. But this?

This was the first time Brooke felt like she was having sex as the woman she was now. And he had said he expected complete honesty, so… "Not right now. Let's leave the bra on."

Flash grinned widely as his hands skimmed up her skin and came to a rest on her shoulders, where he kneaded at the tight muscles there. Clearly, the request didn't bother him in the least. "Can do."

She reached for him again, gripping him firmly as she slid her tongue over his tip and took him into her mouth.

He groaned, a noise of pure desire that traveled down her body to where they were connected. She stroked him with her hands, licked him with her tongue. Suddenly, he pulled away.

"Nope," he growled as he pushed her over.

"Nope?" She flung her hands out for balance as she rolled. His hands pressed between her shoulder blades, firm but not hard. "Did I do something wrong?"

He laughed, a noise that sounded almost unhinged as he gently pushed her onto her stomach. "Wrong? Hell, woman. I've never felt anything so right in my life. But you're about to break me and I'm not going down like that. Not until…"

He stripped her shorts and panties off and Brooke let him. She grabbed handfuls of bedding as he nudged her legs apart and then his hands were between her legs, opening her.

"Woman," he growled again, palming her bottom.

She propped herself up on her elbows and looked back at him. "Not until what?"

"Not until you come first." He trailed his hands over the small of her back, but instead of reaching for that space between her legs that was already hot and heavy for him, he knelt on the bed and rested his hands on her shoulders. His strong hands began to massage her shoulders and she let her head drop as her muscles began to relax. "How much time do we have?"

"An hour, maybe." Bean would wake up from his nap and he'd be hungry and she'd need to nurse him. And then there was dealing with Mom...

"Then we'll make that hour count. Don't think, babe," he said, working at a particularly painful knot. "Just let me take care of you."

His hands moved lower, smoothing over her ribs even as he skipped right over her bra strap. The calluses on his hands chafed at her skin, heightening the sensations, making her more and more aware of his every move, his every touch. She stiffened when he ran his hands over her hips. But then he said, "You are *so* beautiful," in a voice that didn't contain a trace of mockery or teasing in it.

"I'm not back to where I was before," she said, cringing as he traced the stretch marks she'd earned with Bean.

"So?"

She half rolled and shot him a look. "Seriously? Do you know how many people tell me I need to get back to my prebaby weight? My mother, the record execs—they all say the same thing." Her voice cracked a little on the end.

Flash's eyes—well, they flashed. "Let's get one thing straight," he said, rolling her on to her back and pinning her to the bed. "I loved your body last year. I love your body now. But if you think all you are to me is your body and that any variation in your appearance is going to send me running, then you have sorely misjudged how much I need you. All of you."

God, he really was going to make her cry. She tried to wiggle free, but he held her fast.

"So you're not the same person you were then?" he went on, his erection hot and heavy against her thigh, "Well I'm not, either. We've both grown the hell up, Brooke. And, I think, we've both gotten better." Then he released her wrists and moved lower until she felt his lips pressing against those stretch marks, reverently kissing each and every stripe. "You *are* beautiful," he repeated.

Brooke was glad he wasn't staring into her eyes anymore because it wasn't just the compliments. This wasn't Flash being smooth or charming. This was Flash being fierce and proud—of her. This was the man she wanted in her corner, by her side, when record execs tried to railroad her. This was a man who'd fight for her, for their son, for their family.

How had she failed to realize that romance wasn't just pretty words or a sweet song? Because *this* was romance. It was strong and determined and intense. Just like Flash.

Flash looked up from where he was between her legs. "I wanted you a year ago when we were wild kids looking for a good time," he told her. "I want you now when you've had my son and made me a father. A year from now, five years from now, you won't be the same person you are at this exact moment and *I'll still want you*."

Oh, Jesus, that was a hell of a good line, one that fit right into *Don't say something romantic*. He rolled her over again, and this time she let herself relax into his touch. Then one hand slid between her legs, stroking over her sensitive flesh, and the lyrics fell away, only the melody drifting through her mind.

"Yeah, just like that," he said, his voice husky as he touched her, rubbed her, kissed her back. "Don't think. Just feel what I do to you." With his other hand, he pushed her hair to the side and then gripped her neck, gently holding her down while he nipped at her shoulder with his teeth, his stubble scraping over her skin.

Then one finger was inside her and she shuddered at the touch. "Yeah, babe," he breathed in her ear as he worked her body with more patience than she'd ever imagined. Until right now, every time with Flash had been hot and heavy, and neither of them had ever been able to hold back.

But now? Now he was holding himself back, overwhelming her senses and demanding her full attention. She gave it willingly. There was no room for PR plans or redemption stories or albums or should haves, could haves, would haves. There was only him and her and the music that wove their lives together.

Because she'd swear Flash could hear the song, too. With two fingers now, he thrust inside of her in rhythm with the melody as he bit into the skin between her shoulder and her neck. The orgasm began to build and she tried to reach back for him, but he didn't let her go. "You want more?" he growled in her ear, and she heard the raw desire in his voice, felt it in the way his body covered hers, the way her body covered his.

Whimpering, she nodded, and then his hand was gone from her neck, his fingers pulled free of her body. "One sec, babe. Do you have any idea what you do to me?" She peered over her shoulder to see him rolling on the condom. Then he lifted her by the hips and she scooted forward on the bed. "This okay?" he asked, kneeling back on the bed and running his hands over her bottom. "Because I've got to tell you, the view is *amazing*."

She laughed and widened her pose, bracing herself on her elbows. "I seem to recall this was better than okay a year ago." Actually, she remembered the shattering orgasm that had hit her so hard it'd knocked her completely off her knees. She'd been unable to do anything but shake while he'd held her for long, glorious minutes.

No one else had ever made her feel the way Flash did. There were reasons she needed to be careful about him— good reasons, no doubt—but right now, as he fit himself against her, his body strong, she couldn't remember what those reasons were. All she knew was that he was going to make her feel wonderful.

"God, woman," he said, giving her backside a light smack before he thrust into her.

"Oh," she moaned in sheer pleasure as he filled her. Even now, she could feel her orgasm straining against him.

"God, I missed you," he murmured, withdrawing and thrusting back in.

"Yes," she got out, dropping her head onto her forearms on the bed, which gave Flash even more access. He squeezed her bottom and teased her delicate flesh with the softest of touches while he drove into her and she lost herself to the rhythm of their bodies. He'd always been so damn good at this, at making her body react at his mere touch. This was why she couldn't keep her hands off him, couldn't kick him to the curb. She simply needed him too much.

He shifted, reaching around and rubbing her in time with his thrusts, and the pressure built and built, and then he wrapped her hair around his fist and pulled her into him until he could bite down on her shoulder.

The climax hit and crescendoed, her body tightening around his as a cry of satisfaction ripped itself from her chest.

"That's it," he murmured against her skin. "Come for me, babe. Just like… Oh, *God.*"

He reared back, grabbing her hips and thrusting with such force that she couldn't keep her knees underneath her as the sensations completely overwhelmed her. The orgasm went on, strengthening until she cried out again.

Seconds later, Flash made a noise of raw lust and collapsed onto her back, driving her into the bed. He managed to roll off to one side, his arm and leg still draped over her. She didn't know how long they lay there, panting, but soon enough the heat from their bodies dissipated and she shivered.

"Oh, babe," Flash sighed, wrapping himself around her and holding on tight. "I…"

She didn't know how he was going to finish that sentence. *Say something romantic*. This time, her brain modulated the key up to A.

No, no—she didn't want him to say something romantic. She didn't want him to make her fall for him all over again, didn't want him to propose when she was weak for him because, after sex like that, she might just say yes.

She just wanted to enjoy him while she could, which she had. Now she needed to focus on reality.

She rolled away from him and out of bed. "I'm still not marrying you," she tossed over her shoulder as she walked—okay, hurried—to the bathroom.

She shut the door before he could answer.

Twelve

She wasn't going to make this easy on him, that much was clear.

While Brooke got cleaned up, Flash flopped across the bed, trying to get his thoughts in order. He wanted nothing more than to pull her right back into bed, curl around her body and nap the rest of the afternoon away, but they didn't have that much time. Not yet, anyway.

Okay, he could do this. He was calm, cool and collected and, thanks to the amazing sex, he could think without getting distracted by her body or his dick. Probably.

First things first—tea.

Just because he wanted her in ways that continually surprised him didn't mean she was his. And it especially didn't mean that he was over her hiding James from him. All it meant was they were…exploring areas of consensus or some such BS.

He launched himself out of bed, disposed of the condom and hurriedly washed his hands in the kitchen. Then he assembled her tea. The water had cooled a little, but it was still hot enough, he hoped. Then he squeezed in a dollop of honey. There.

She still didn't want to get married. She'd made it crystal clear before she'd come over here that she wasn't going to marry him. What he needed to figure out was if she was digging in her heels because he'd pushed too far, too fast or if, when she said she wasn't going to marry him, she was really saying *not right now*. And the sooner he figured that out, the better off they'd all be.

He made it back to the bedroom just as the bathroom door opened. Brooke walked into the bedroom in all her glory, and he was so stunned by her that he damn near dropped the mug. "Babe," he all but groaned, his body straining to muster a response.

She crossed her arms in front of her breasts, still teasingly contained by that pretty bra. "Focus, Flash. We have to talk."

"Right, right." He let his gaze travel down her body, taking in every curve and dip. "Are we talking with or without clothes? I vote without."

"Of course you do." She sighed, but she smiled while she said it. "Is that tea?"

"Jasmine green tea with honey." He held out the tea, making sure not to touch her.

Which was harder than anticipated when she took the mug from him, that satisfied smile on her lips. He'd put that smile there, and he'd do whatever it took to replace it with another one. If she'd let him, he'd make sure she smiled like that every day for the rest of their lives.

Then she frowned and he realized that she wasn't scowling at the tea, but at his hands. His swollen, red hands. "Is that from hitting couch cushions?"

Flash flexed his fingers, wincing. He didn't like that note of doubt in her voice. "Nope. This morning I found a boxing club that let me punch a bag for an hour." He'd had to buy a year's membership, but that hadn't bothered him a bit. Nashville was where Brooke was—her family, her career, her life. He'd be back in town. Often.

Luckily, the boxing club had been three blocks from a jeweler's shop, so he'd been able to kill two birds with one stone, so to speak. The ring itself had seven stones. God, he hoped she liked it.

Brooke looked worried. "And that helps?"

"Absolutely. I have a bag at home, too," he added. "Like I said last night—it's a controlled release. I haven't been in a fight in months."

"Do you remember what it was about?" Clearly, she expected the answer to be *no*.

But he did. "I got into it with Pete right before he and Chloe got hitched—and I was stone-cold sober when I did it. I thought I was protecting my sister, but Chloe let me know in no uncertain terms that she did not need my protection and that I was a jackass for thinking she'd ever want my help." He chuckled, rubbing a hand over his jaw. "Pete'll never let me forget that he broke my jaw. Of course, my face is pretty hard. I broke his hand, so we were even."

She gaped at him. "Seriously?"

"Seriously. I went cold turkey after that—had to. My hands were a mess and my jaw was wired shut for a while. But that was the wake-up call I needed. I almost cost my sister everything she loves, almost ruined my entire career and came damn close to destroying the All-Stars—not to mention risking jail time—all because I couldn't get a handle on my temper."

The thing that still boggled his mind was how damned sure he'd been at the time. When he'd overheard Tex Mc-Graw making horribly crude comments about Brooke, Flash had known he'd needed to defend her honor. That had gotten him arrested and nearly sent to prison. And when he'd gone after Pete, he'd been convinced that the man was taking advantage of Chloe. He'd been positive he'd been right both times.

Now? Now he could see that neither woman had needed his protection. Brooke probably didn't even know Tex existed, much less that he was a sexist jerk. Chloe had been able to handle Pete and the All-Stars just fine on her own. The only thing Flash had ever done was make things worse.

It'd been a hell of a hard lesson to learn but he was learning it. Yeah, last night he'd been 100 percent sure that Brooke needed to marry him immediately, and because of that he'd almost destroyed any chance at a real relationship with her.

"And you're telling me you have a handle on that anger now? That you and Pete are...friends?" Skepticism dripped off every word.

Flash took a deep breath. It was all right if she was skeptical. She'd had months with those headlines eating at her. It would be unreasonable for her to nod and smile and pretend his past didn't bother her at all, especially after last night.

"We get by. And he treats my sister right." He cleared his throat. "Just so you know, I called Oliver, my brother. I told him about James, but not who you were." Although Oliver had figured it out, no doubt. He wasn't the one running the family's energy company by accident.

"I met him, right?"

"I think so, at the Fort Worth rodeo. Oliver's the oldest. He runs Lawrence Energies, which is the family business. He's married to Renee and they have an eight-month-old daughter, Trixie. My dad doesn't run the company anymore."

"Are you really a billionaire?"

"Me, personally? Probably not. Why?"

Brooke's eyes about bugged out of her head. "*Probably* not? You're not sure?"

"I sold my stake in Lawrence Energies when I started riding in the All-Stars to avoid the conflicts of interest. Invested most of it, blew some of it on cars and horses. Bought a nice piece of land a few hours south of Dallas with a big ol' house on it—plenty of room for a boy to have a good time," he added. "I get statements from the brokers, but I don't really read them."

Brooke clutched her tea like it was a life preserver and she was trying not to drown. "You don't even know..." she said quietly.

Flash took advantage of this to climb into bed behind her. He sat in the middle and pulled the sheets up over his waist.

He wasn't going to win the fight to not touch her. As softly as he could, he skimmed his hand over her back. She didn't lean away from him, so that had to count for something. "Is it a problem?"

"No, no. It's just... I didn't grow up rich, and then my uncle stole most of my money or lost it, and..." Her voice trailed off as she focused on him. "And, in the interests of honesty, part of what set me off last night was your sister implying that your family had the money to take me to court and bleed me dry if I didn't cooperate."

Flash groaned. "Yeah, I can see how that'd be upsetting," he said, closing his eyes and pushing back against the frustration. The whole point of calling his sister was so she would *help*, not freak Brooke the hell out! "Sorry about that. The point she should've made was that if you have any outstanding bills for his care or if he needs anything else—diapers or, uh, strollers?" Honestly, he had no idea what a baby would need. "Definitely a pony when he gets old enough."

Brooke grinned at his cluelessness although at least she was trying to hide it behind the mug.

"Or whatever—it's covered," Flash went on. "If there's

anything *you* need, just let me know." He tried to think—what would she want? Then it hit him. "Aside from all the tea you could drink, if you want a recording studio at my place, I'll get one built. If you decide you want a different house, one we share, I'll get it—with your name on the title. I'll start a trust fund for James, too, for college or whatever."

She blinked at him. "You'd build me a studio?"

"Hell, yeah." Actually, the more he thought about it, the better he liked that idea. Brooke could stay for weeks or even months. She could work on her music while Flash taught James how to ride and take care of his pony or took him to a rodeo. Then she wouldn't be tied to Nashville. Although they'd maintain a residence here because obviously Brooke would need to come back here on a regular basis. "I can get contractors started on it next week." He didn't actually know what went into a recording studio, but, hell, money wasn't an object. He'd hire someone who did know and tell them to get top-of-the-line equipment. Problem solved.

"That..." She actually blushed. "That would be lovely."

Yeah, that was exactly how he would show her he was good for her. "But the point is, you've already done the hard part. I want to make things easy for you from here on out, and I don't want the money differences to be a wedge between us."

"I appreciate that." She took a long drink. "Anything else I should know about your family?"

He shrugged. "You've met Chloe, who runs the All-Stars, which used to be part of Lawrence Energies, but now she owns it outright. And me." He launched a self-deprecating grin at her. "I don't run anything."

"But you're one of the best all-around rodeo riders in the world," she said, which had him puffing out his chest a little.

"I try. We haven't told Dad yet because subtlety isn't his strong suit, especially when it comes to grandbabies." Point of fact, the man had gone hog-wild for Trixie, all the more so because Oliver and Renee had named the baby after his beloved wife. It's not like that little girl wanted for anything—Oliver was much better at the whole money thing than Flash would ever be. But every time Milt Lawrence saw his granddaughter, he had another toy, another frilly dress, another keepsake present just for her. The man was over the moon.

"What about your mom? Is she still in the picture?"

Flash swallowed hard as he stroked her back. "She died when I was eleven."

Brooke gasped. "I'm so sorry. I hadn't realized."

"It's okay," he said with the casual shrug he always used when talking about his mom. He was used to her being gone, anyway. That was practically the same thing as it being okay. "I know now that everyone did a lot to shield me from the chaos, but, obviously, everything changed when she lost her fight with cancer."

Mom would've loved Brooke. And there would've been no getting her away from James. She would've known if Flash was doing the right thing. She would've loved her grandson, would've protected Brooke as if she were her own daughter. Trixie Lawrence would've made everything about this better. Flash didn't often miss her—she'd been gone more than half his life—but right now, he missed his mom.

"I'm sorry to hear that," she sniffed, wrapping her arms around his chest and hugging him back.

"It's okay. It was a long time ago. Right after that, Dad won the All-Stars in a poker game and relocated the entire family to Dallas. He couldn't stay in New York where we'd lived with Mom, so we all moved. He started going to rodeos and hanging out with cowboys, and he took me with him. And I learned real quick that there were two kinds of guys at those things—those who were quick with a wink and a joke and those who were quick with their fists."

Dad would disappear to go play cards with his buddies, shooting the breeze and drinking, leaving Flash to run wild. Chloe was usually at the rodeos with them, and she been charged with keeping an eye on him, but Flash had insisted that he hadn't needed a babysitter and had ditched her whenever he could.

"That's where I got my nickname," he told Brooke. "I was small and quick, and I could get into trouble and then disappear—" he snapped his fingers for emphasis "—in a *flash*."

He'd always looked back at his childhood with such fondness. What kid didn't love doing whatever he damn well pleased? But now Flash wondered how things might have been different if Milt Lawrence hadn't been in the grips of a midlife crisis and deep depression following the loss of his beloved wife. Would Flash be a different man today if his father had shown him how to be a different man then?

Brooke sniffed again. "I don't know that I realized you hadn't grown up on a ranch somewhere. You're such a quintessential cowboy."

"I'll take that as a compliment, but I was a city slicker kid from New York."

She curled against his side, and it only made sense for him to drape his arm around her shoulder and hug her close. This was…nice.

"But my point is, for most of my life, I only knew how to be one of two people—a ladies' man who sweet-talked all the pretty girls or a fighter who refused to back down. But when I'm with you, I don't have to stay stuck in those two extremes. I can be someone else."

"Oh, *Flash*," she whispered, looking up at him. He wiped a lingering tear from her cheek.

"I need to be in my son's life on a regular basis," he told her. "And I think it's pretty clear that sex between you and me is gonna be a thing."

"A *good* thing," she murmured, not sounding happy about it. "It'd be easier if it wasn't."

Yeah, if he could keep his hands off her, it'd make what was supposed to be a negotiation more cut-and-dried.

But he couldn't keep his hands off her, as evidenced by the way he stroked her back. "What about your family?"

She shrugged, but he felt the tension ripple through her body. "It's me and Mom. I don't know who my dad was— Mom refuses to talk about him."

"Really?"

"Oh, yeah," she said, slumping back against the bed. "She won't tell me a damn thing about my father, but yet she's been pushing me to sign off on a big baby reveal. Plus, she refuses to see how much of a hypocrite she's being about it. All she can say is it isn't the same—because why? Because I've got a music career? It's BS. Mom is very... focused," she explained. "She pushed me into a singing career from when I was in kindergarten. Which wasn't bad," she added, maybe a little too quickly.

Flash was getting a mental image of her mother that was anything but flattering. The woman sounded domineering, controlling and more than just a little mean. "Are you sure about that?"

She nodded. "I love what I do and I've had some great friends."

"Like Kyle Morgan?" Flash hadn't forgotten the way the older man had given Flash a mean look.

"Yeah, Kyle's been a great mentor. But even the best mentor isn't a replacement for a father. I don't even know if my dad knows I exist and I *hate* it. I've always hated it.

I can't help wondering if he didn't want me." She leaned against him as she said it.

Flash's mind reeled even as he held her tight. True, he'd always butted heads with his father—but he'd always known how much he was loved. His heart hurt for Brooke, for the pain in her voice.

"That's on him," Flash said, furious with this random sperm donor. "Not you, babe. And I would never do that to my child. Even if *this* doesn't work out between you and me, I'm not abandoning my kid. He's a Lawrence no matter what."

She exhaled heavily. "Good. That's good. You know, I'd made peace with it, with her and with him," Brooke went on, her voice small. "Or I thought I had. Then you happened and I got pregnant and it brought it all home—how much Mom kept hidden from me. I love her, but I don't know if I can ever forgive her. Does that make sense?"

Flash felt like she'd punched him. "Yeah," he got out in a strangled voice. "I understand completely."

Because he felt exactly the same way. He cared for Brooke, more than he probably should. And he felt such a powerful, instinctual love for James that he couldn't even put it into words.

But how would he get past the fact that Brooke had kept that baby boy a secret from Flash? Was forgiveness even possible?

"And it was so hard not to call you up and tell you then," she went on, seemingly unaware that she'd just blown Flash's mind. "You've got to believe me, Flash—I always meant to tell you. I never intended to keep you from Bean or him from you. Because I know it's not right. I was just…"

"Waiting for the right time," he said softly after she'd trailed off.

"Yeah." She swallowed. "I wish I'd realized that the right time was actually a few months ago."

That made two of them.

"I'm not going to be like her," she said, her voice stronger as she sat up straighter. "I want Bean to know you and your family. I want us to get to a point where we can make some version of *this* work."

Flash had to swallow a few times. "Yeah, me too."

She tapped a pattern on the tea mug. "The question is, how do we make that happen?"

He scratched a hand through his hair. "The general consensus is that me telling you we *had* to get hitched was the dumbest thing I've done in a long, long time."

"So why did you do it?"

He kept his gaze locked on her face. "*Because*. Which—" he added with a chuckle when her lips twisted off to the side in disapproval "—is a bad answer. I've learned that. But the truth is, you mean something to me, Brooke."

He felt, more than saw, the eye roll. He tried again. "From the moment I laid eyes on you, I haven't looked at another woman—and that's not just a figure of speech. There's something between us, and it's got the potential to be something good. Something great, even. But," he went on before she could tell him where he could shove all his *potential*, "that doesn't mean we make sense married. We both have careers that require near-constant travel, and there's a lot riding on us doing our jobs well."

"That's true," she admitted, sounding almost regretful about it. "I'm not giving up my music."

"Which is absolutely fair. You've been the front line for a year. More than a year," he said. "Have you done it alone?"

She didn't meet his gaze. Instead, her fingers continued to tap out a rhythm on her mug. "I've got Alex. And my mother. She's with Bean now. I may not agree with all of her *choices*, as you put it, but she loves him completely." She winced, her fingers stilling as she shot him an apologetic look. "She'll like you even less than Alex does."

Every single time, Brooke's statements about her mother had been couched in worry and maybe a little bit of fear. If Mrs. Bonner was James's primary babysitter, that probably meant Brooke had needed the time between when she'd left the Bluebird and when Flash had shown up at her house to get her mother out of her house.

Mrs. Bonner was a problem.

Oliver had made it clear why Flash needed to establish paternity immediately, if not sooner. For once, Flash and Oliver had been in agreement about something—marriage would make everything smoother.

Smoother for the Lawrences, yeah. But for Brooke? She needed more than that and, by God, Flash wanted to be the one to give it to her.

"I'm not worried about your mom. I'm worried about *you*." He stroked his thumb over her cheek. Unexpectedly, her eyes began to water. "You impress the hell out of me, you know? You toured while pregnant and had our baby and still wrote a bunch of kick-ass songs. You've done such an amazing job, and I couldn't ask for a better mother for my son."

"Damn it," she sniffed, pulling away from his touch and swiping at her eyes. "Don't be charming, Flash. I'm too tired to cope with you being perfect."

"I'm not being charming," he told her as he put her almost empty mug on the nightstand and then lifted her into his lap. "I'm being honest. I'll always be honest with you. Just be honest with me, too. That's all I ask."

Crying, she settled into his lap, her arms around his neck. This wasn't sexual, although there was no missing the fact that there was little more than a sheet between their nude bodies.

No, this was him taking care of her. He wrapped his arms around her, and relief coursed through him when she rested her head on his shoulder. Leaning back against the headboard, he let his body take her weight while he stroked her back and kissed her forehead and let her get it all out.

Long minutes passed, and he didn't think about her mother or his family or songs or rodeos or anything but this woman.

He wanted her.

It really didn't make sense, except it did. He'd wanted her a year ago and he wanted her now. Would he still want her in another year?

Would she still want him?

It was a huge risk. But, hell, he was Flash Lawrence. Everything he did was a risk.

"Anything between us has to start from trust, and I…" He swallowed hard. "I understand why you did what you did. But I don't trust you as much as I need to right now, and you probably don't trust me as much as you need to, either." She gasped, but he didn't stop. He couldn't. "I'm not going to get it right all the time. I didn't last night. But that doesn't mean I'm going to stop trying."

Another tear trickled down her cheek and he wiped this one away, too. "You're being perfect again," she said in what might have been a scolding voice if it hadn't been so choked with emotion.

"Trying to be, anyway," he said. She laughed, and she was so beautiful, a smile on her face even as tears clung to her eyelashes, that he kissed her. His body surged to attention as he held her tight.

He could get lost in the honeyed sweetness of this woman, and that thought made him realize something— he did want to marry her. It might be a disaster and it'd definitely be messy but…

His father still talked about how he'd taken one look at Trixie Cunningham and that'd been it for him. In the years since her death, he'd never dated, never taken a lover. He was still in love with his wife. She'd been the only woman for him.

How was that different from how Flash had reacted to Brooke? He'd laid eyes on her at the All-Stars Rodeo in Fort Worth and he hadn't stopped thinking about Brooke, hadn't touched another woman, since then.

What if this was the same thing?

What if this was forever?

Thirteen

She pulled away, resting her head on his shoulder again. "We don't have much time."

"Right." Damn it. He tried to get his mind back on track. "Okay. We need a plan."

"Yes. Definitely a plan." But then she gave him a dreamy smile and kissed him again.

She was absolutely *killing* him, but what a way to go. "First things first—what do *you* want to do?"

That dreaminess faded, replaced by a worried furrow between her brows. "You know, I don't think anyone's ever asked."

Flash winced. Yeah, he'd skipped that step last night. "We need to find a workable solution. And that may or may not involve marriage. So be honest."

She was quiet for a long time, but Flash held himself still, and finally she began to talk. "I don't want to use my child as leverage. I want people to see him as a person in his own right instead of a marketing tool. I want to take him to parks and the zoo and introduce him to my friends—who'll all be mad that I've lied to them for the last year. I don't want to lie anymore. I want to feel like I'm in control of at least some part of my own life."

"That all sounds good to me," he said softly. He didn't want to interrupt her.

"I don't want to be forced into anything, like I was when my mother and my record company made the executive decision to hide my pregnancy," she went on. "I don't want to be made to feel ashamed of who I am or who Bean is. I want my new album to do well, and I want to do a smaller, more manageable tour that won't be so exhausting. I want to keep my son with me and I want…" Her gaze cut to him and he hoped like hell he saw desire there.

He leaned forward, hoping to catch that last word, hoping it was *you*.

As her words trailed off, she rolled onto her side and stared at him. "I want to be friends with you, because I like you, too." Her tone was suddenly diplomatic. Was she being honest? "I want to know you better, and you're right—I want to trust you more than I do now. I want Bean to know his whole family. I want everything to be perfect."

She didn't say *not like this*, but Flash heard it anyway.

"That's quite a list."

She swiped at her eyes again. "Yeah. Not going to apologize for any of it."

He could sense the frustration underneath every request—the long nights, the loneliness, the worry that underscored her every moment, and it wrecked him that he hadn't been here for her.

The truth was that he'd nearly ruined his entire life because he'd had some dumb-ass idea that attacking another guy for daring to talk about her was protecting her, but it wasn't. Truly protecting her would've been standing by her side for the last year, backing her up when she'd needed to push against her mother or her record label, holding her hand during labor, being there for the sleepless nights.

He couldn't change the past. The important thing was that she didn't see herself on opposite sides of him or his family. Everything else, he could work with. He wanted her to keep writing, keep singing, and if she wanted to tour, he'd make it work.

Mrs. Bonner was *definitely* going to be a problem, though. Because if there was one thing Flash understood, it was being an adult who everyone still treated like a kid.

He leaned over and pulled the ring box out of the drawer where he'd stashed it when she'd called. "Brooke."

Her eyes went wide as she scrambled into a sitting position—one where she wasn't touching him. "Flash, don't do this."

"I'm not proposing—promise," he corrected quickly. He set the box down in the no-man's land between them. "Let's call it a…business partnership."

She eyed him warily. He hated that look, hated that she still felt she had to guard herself against him. "What kind of partnership?"

"Several things need to happen." Things he'd discussed with Chloe and Pete last night and again with Oliver this morning. At least Oliver had only yelled for a few minutes, although there had been that threat of permanent dismemberment…

"We need a paternity test, for starters. Not because I doubt you," he said, which made her roll her eyes. "Anyone who looks at that boy knows he's mine." Chloe had said as much.

"You do have the same smile," she said quietly, giving him a grin that was almost shy.

"We need the test, because I'm not on the birth certificate and I don't want anyone else to question the fact that he's my son." Anyone like her mother, specifically.

Brooke blew out a long breath. "Yes, of course. There's no question about that."

"Good." The next part, however, was trickier. Chloe had told him what she and Brooke had talked about—including how Chloe had gotten distracted by the baby and started thinking out loud about how they were going to sell this to the public. Flash had called her because he wasn't good at big-picture thinking like that, but he also completely understood why it'd overwhelmed Brooke.

"Have you thought about what Chloe mentioned last night? Before the cushion incident?"

Brooke slumped back onto the bed, her fingers tapping a rhythm only she could hear. Flash was sure she didn't know she was doing it.

"Yes," she said quietly, not looking at him. "It's not a bad plan. It's definitely the kind of thing the record label will sign off on, especially when your name gets out there. But I don't want to get married, you know?"

"Okay. Got that." He'd have to be dead to miss it.

"So what is this?" she asked, nudging the box. "How is a ring—it is a ring, right?" Flash nodded. "How is a ring a business proposal?"

He thought back to that list of things she wanted out of their relationship. The good news was she wanted to be friends with him. Friends spent time together. They hung out, went out, called and texted and sent pictures. Sometimes, friends even stripped each other naked and had extremely satisfying sex.

But she'd also didn't want her choices taken away, and she didn't want to feel ashamed. "Chloe said she could spin our relationship so you're in the driver's seat. We were dating and you got pregnant and then I screwed up and you gave me an ultimatum to shape up or ship out, which I did. Right?"

"Basically…" She crossed her arms and stared at the jeweler's box as if it held the Ring of Sauron or something.

"So we could get engaged." He opened the box, the huge diamond surrounded by sapphires, all catching the light. Brooke gasped in what he hoped was approval.

"Holy crap—look at the size of that rock!" she whispered. Then she looked up at him, her eyes huge. "Engaged? Are you asking me to marry you again?"

Flash took that to be a sign that he'd chosen well. "Nope." She snorted, but her gaze fell back to the ring. "We don't have to set a date, much less book the band and send out invitations. Chloe said we'd tell people we'd be keeping it quiet, like our whole relationship. Then, in a year or whenever, we could break up, ask for privacy during our difficult time, and promise that we would continue to put our child first. And none of that would be a lie, necessarily." Although the thought of her moving on, falling in love with someone else who'd get to spend time raising his son— yeah, that rankled.

"You're serious," she said, sounding breathless. She stretched out a finger toward the ring before she snatched it back, like the ring might burn her.

"Yep." Months of a friendly fake engagement gave Flash room to work. He could take her—and James, of course— out. He could demonstrate he had the chops to be a good father and, most importantly, that he was trustworthy—all without screwing up his big championship year.

Hopefully, during that time, he could get to a point where he could trust her, too. He knew that was a ways off, but he didn't want to spend the rest of his life questioning her every statement or action, either.

And if they were together, it only made sense that they might spend some time in bed, right?

"You can tour for your new album, I can still ride the rodeo on the weekends and, when we can, we make time to work on this parenting thing." He laughed nervously. "I need more work than you do, I reckon."

"And I could call it off whenever I wanted?" she asked softly. This time, she did pick up the ring, studying the huge round-cut diamond.

Yeah, he'd made the right choice. "Of course. You could do that even if it were a real engagement."

"You won't ask me to marry you again?"

He chuckled. "Nope. The offer stands, though." He took the ring from her. "I guessed on the size." He held out his hand for hers.

She made him wait for it, which he probably deserved. "This is the last moment before everything changes. *Again*," she murmured. "After this, it'll be out of our hands."

"No, it won't," he promised, pulling her into a hug. "I won't let anyone run you down. We're in this together."

"What about sex?" she murmured against his bare shoulder.

His pulse stuttered at the thought. "I'm not about to step out on you. The only thing I ask is that you do the same. And…" He had to dig deep to get the words out. "And if we go our separate ways, I want to meet whoever you date before you introduce him to our son."

She nodded against him and said, "Like I have time to date, anyway."

"Yeah," he agreed, letting his hands roam down her back. "I'm going to be busy for the foreseeable future." He had a championship to win, a kid to father and Brooke…

Yeah, he was going to have his hands *full*. "If you want sex to be a part of this *whatever* it is we're going to do, then I'm okay with that." That was the freaking understatement of the century. Just having this conversation was making him hard for her all over again. "If you don't want to be physical, that's okay, too. I still won't sleep with anyone else."

She sighed. "I think...no, I *know* that if we're going to be around each other, we're going to wind up just like this, whether we plan on it or not."

She pulled away and Flash managed not to groan in frustration, so score one for maturity. Damned maturity.

"If we're engaged," she went on, finality in her voice. "I wouldn't want to say it's fake, because I like you, and *this*," she said, motioning between their bodies, "is very, *very* good."

"Happy to hear," he replied, waggling his eyebrows suggestively.

Was she agreeing?

She was.

Taking a deep breath, she squared her shoulders and held out her left hand, palm down. "Okay," she said, sounding for all the world like she was gearing up for battle, not accepting his ring. "Let's do this. For Bean."

"For *us*." Flash didn't realize his own hands were shaking until he slid the diamond onto her finger. "Whatever happens," he told her, his voice low and serious, "we're in this together. Trust me."

The ring fit.

A part of his mind wanted to say it was fate, that she was meant to be his and he would always be hers.

She stared at his ring on her finger. "Trust..." She sighed heavily. A little too heavily. "Because nothing says *trustworthy* like an only sort-of-real engagement, right?"

"It's a challenge," he told her. One that involved working together as a team, developing a physical connection and, *far* down the line, the chance to win it all.

Being almost really engaged to Brooke Bonner was not unlike riding in a rodeo, frankly.

This was Flash's year, and Brooke Bonner was the biggest challenge of his life.

Fourteen

Things happened very quickly after Brooke managed to pull herself out of Flash's arms and out of his bed.

First, she called Alex and updated her friend on the new plan. Not unsurprisingly, Alex wasn't a huge fan of the plan. Or of Flash. "*Engaged?* Seriously? I'm not sure this is the best idea."

"You got a better one?" Brooke shot back. "I can't keep hiding, Alex. You know I can't. It's not right. And, yes, it's going to suck for a while, but it was always going to suck. We just delayed the suckiness."

"Yeah, yeah, I know." Another longish pause. "You going to marry him?"

"We're *engaged.*" Which wasn't really an answer to that question, but it was the only one she was going to give to Alex, to her mother, to the press. They were engaged. Period. End of discussion.

"I'll break him if he hurts you," she growled into the phone.

Brooke laughed it off because how else was she supposed to respond to what was probably a serious threat?

"I'll fill you in on all the details later." Alex made what

sounded a lot like a retching noise. "But the main thing right now is that we're going to bring Bean to the All-Stars Rodeo Friday night and I hope you'll be able to be there. It'd mean a lot to me." Flash gave her a thumbs-up. "To both of us."

Alex, however, was in no mood to be charmed. "I'm not gonna like him, so quit trying," she snapped, but, in true Alex form, she softened immediately. "Okay, fine. We're all going to the rodeo. Have you told your mom yet?"

"No, that's next. We're going out to the house after this," Brooke said.

"Well, good luck with *that*." She hung up.

Some of Flash's good humor faded. "That didn't sound good."

"It's not." There were no words to describe how little Brooke was looking forward to this introduction.

Flash kissed her forehead before saying, "However you want to handle it is how we'll handle it. I'm here to back you up."

She couldn't help the sigh of relief that escaped her. This was the Flash she wanted. Perfect and charming and thoughtful and beside her. Not out in front, not trying to take over, but supporting her. "Just…maybe focus on demonstrating you're a good father? For all our issues, she does love Bean."

If he tried to charm Mom outright, it'd be a disaster. But if he could convince Crissy Bonner that he'd take good care of her grandson, then maybe it wouldn't be too bad.

"That I can do," he promised, pulling her to her feet and brushing a kiss over her lips, then her cheek. "And then afterwards?"

The next kiss was anything but soft or sweet, and maybe it wasn't the smartest thing to do, but Brooke let herself be swept away by his heat, his taste.

"Will you stay tonight?" she whispered against his

mouth. She could sleep in his arms and maybe he could at least get up with Bean, even if she'd still have to nurse him. And if they were already sharing a bed… "Will you stay with me?"

He touched his forehead to hers, his thumbs stroking over her cheeks. "For as long as you'll let me, babe."

She chose not to think about what he was really saying.

Forty minutes later, Brooke was pretty sure she'd made a tactical error bringing Flash home with her unannounced.

"*Who* is this?" Mom demanded, clutching Bean to her chest as she eyed Flash suspiciously. The look in her eyes promised a storm was about to be unleashed.

But Brooke wasn't going to back down. Not this time. Not ever again.

Mother might know best, but Brooke was a mother now, too. And she knew what was best for her family.

She glanced at Flash. He was family now, especially when he gave her hand an encouraging squeeze and shot her a little wink. Then he turned the full power of his charming smile back to her mother and said, "Mrs. Bonner, I'm Frasier Lawrence. My family owns Lawrence Energies in Dallas." Then, because he was Flash, he threw in a little bow. "I'm Bean's father and," he continued smoothly over Mom's gasp of horror, "I've asked your daughter to marry me." He lifted Brooke's hand and kissed her knuckle, right above the simply huge diamond engagement ring.

She noted that Flash carefully avoided the lie that Brooke had agreed to be his wife. He simply let the jewelry and his real name do the talking for him.

The noise Mom made was barely human. "You *what*? Who the hell *is* this?"

She startled poor Bean, who definitely hadn't recovered from all the excitement the night before. He promptly melted down.

"Now look what you've done!" Mom yelled at Flash over the baby's wails. Bean cried louder.

Brooke tensed because if Flash was going to lose his temper, this would be the moment when it happened.

He didn't. Instead, Flash simply squeezed Brooke's hand and focused on Mom. "Ma'am, I think my son is hungry. Let me check his diaper before I give him to Brooke." He plucked the baby out of Mom's stunned arms. "Hey, honey. I heard you let Mommy sleep a little last night," he cooed to the baby as he headed for the stairs. He shifted so Bean was tucked against his shoulder. "Maybe we'll let her get some more sleep tonight. Won't that be great? Yeah, that's my good boy."

Bean, bless his heart, managed a wobbly grin, even as he gave Brooke a worried look. But he let Flash carry him upstairs.

Brooke's heart clenched with a fierce need because, yeah, he was putting on a show for Mom, but, God, the sight of him cuddling his son, of Bean responding to him— that was what she needed from him. *She* needed to know he'd be a good father.

"You're getting married?" Mom asked, not bothering to wait until Flash and Bean were out of earshot.

"Not today," Brooke replied. "But Flash—that's Frasier's nickname—and I are going to—"

"Wait—that's *Flash* Lawrence?" Mom interrupted, the blood draining from her face. "The criminal?"

"Actually, he's a rodeo rider." Brooke took a cue from Flash and counted her breaths for a moment until she was sure she had her temper under control. "I don't expect you to understand or approve, Mom."

"You're damn right I don't," she fired back. "Do you have any idea what he's capable of? He will destroy your career." With great physical effort, Mom attempted to look caring. She didn't come close. "Honey, let's think about this. I'm just not sure this *marriage*," she said, like the word tasted bad in her mouth, "is for the best, you know? We've kept his…contribution quiet for this long. There's no reason to break that silence right now." She shot Brooke the look that normally had her dropping her gaze, unwilling to risk further angering Crissy Bonner. But then her mother added, "You know I just want what's best for your career," in what was probably supposed to be a gentle voice, except it came out as an order.

Right. If Mom was truly worried about Flash's "criminal" history, she'd be worried about Brooke or about Bean. But it always came back to the career with Crissy Bonner.

Brooke ignored the sting of rejection layered within her mother's words. "He can't be any worse for my career than your brother was when he stole all my money and disappeared to Mexico," Brooke shot back. "But you convinced me that hiring Uncle Brantley was 'for the best' because it kept my career in the family, right?"

"He's my brother," Mom snapped. "I trusted him, too. It's not my fault he made poor choices. Just like it's not my fault you made poor choices!"

"Do *not* call my child a poor choice," Brooke seethed.

"All I'm trying to do is contain the damage," Mom went on. "And until we know what that man's motivations are, it's for the best to keep him out of the picture. That doesn't make me the bad guy here!"

"Oh? Just like you kept my father out of the picture?"

Mom had already opened her mouth to fire back another excuse, but at Brooke's words, her jaw snapped shut. "You have no idea what you're talking about," she said in a dangerous whisper.

"Of course I don't—because you won't tell me!" Brooke was shouting now, but she didn't care. Years of resentments bubbled up and poured out. "For God's sake, Mom, I'm not a little girl anymore! I'm a woman, and I'm more than capable of deciding what I need to be protected from. Or were you just protecting yourself?" The words came flying out of her mouth before she could stop them. "Maybe you were just afraid that, if I knew my father, I'd choose him over you!"

True hurt flashed over her mother's face, but it was gone in an instant. "After all I've done for you, this is how you repay me?"

That line might've worked on Brooke when she was a teenager, but she wasn't about to fall for that guilt trip now. "Who was he, Mom?"

Everything about Crissy Bonner screamed, *Not telling*, from the tight line of her mouth to the way she'd crossed her arms in front of her.

"Don't you think I deserve to know? At least for Bean's sake. What if there are medical issues we should know about?"

"This discussion is over," Mom snapped. She made a move toward the door.

Brooke blocked her. Somehow, she knew that if Mom walked out that door, she'd never get answers. "I've let you keep your secrets for years, but you owe me this. You made sure I grew up without knowing anything about my father. If you think I'm going to let you do the exact same thing to Bean, then you've underestimated how far I'll go to protect him!"

"You foolish girl—did you ever consider the fact that maybe *he* didn't want you to know who he was?"

"Of course I did." It didn't take a big mental leap to figure that her father simply didn't want her, because if he did, he'd have found a way to be with her. "But does that justify lying to me my entire life?"

Mom tried to push past her, but Brooke wasn't having any of it. She grabbed her mom by her shoulders and demanded, "Who was he?"

"This is a mistake," Mom hissed. She twisted out of Brooke's grasp and made a turn, probably heading for the back door.

Brooke snatched her hand and held tight. "Mom, please. It won't make me love you any less." Who knew, maybe it'd help her understand her mother's *unique* kind of love even more. "Promise."

"You really think I haven't told you just because I'm embarrassed or something? Fine. But you take this up with him. I wash my hands of this whole mess."

"Fine?" Was Crissy Bonner actually going to tell the truth? And Brooke wasn't entirely sure what Mom meant with that *mess* comment. "Who?"

"Kyle Morgan," she snapped. "There. Happy?"

"Kyle? *Kyle?*" Brooke's old friend? The man who'd taught her how to write a song, who'd given her a guitar for her eleventh birthday? Who'd been there the night of her first show at the Bluebird and helped her land her record deal? The man who'd threatened Flash behind the Bluebird?

Kyle Morgan was her father.

And he'd never told her.

"Does he…does he know? Who I am?"

"Of course he does, not that it ever mattered to him. But just because Kyle cut and ran doesn't mean you have to marry *that* man," Mom went on, wrenching her hand away from Brooke and pointing to the second floor. "You've already made one mistake. Two wrongs don't make a right. Trust me on *that*, Brooke."

Numbly, Brooke looked up to see Flash standing at the top of the stairs, Bean in his arms. "Brooke?" he said softly into the eerie silence that settled in the space between Brooke and her mother. "We're ready for you."

She was not going to cry in front of her mother. She was not going to rant and rave and demand to know what the hell Mom and Kyle had been thinking. She was not going to lose it completely. She simply wasn't.

Suddenly she understood why Flash had been punching couch cushions.

"I will cut you out of Bean's life if you ever refer to him as a mistake again," Brooke said, her voice unnaturally calm. "Flash and I are engaged. He's Bean's father and we're together now. And I think it'd be best if I found a manager who understood the difference between managing my career and managing me. I love you, Mom, but I don't know how I'm going to forgive you for this. Or Kyle."

A muscle twitched on Mom's forehead. "Fine. You're on your own."

"Fine." Actually, it was a relief. She was zero-for-two with family members as managers. "Thank you for watching Bean today."

"His name is Jimmy," Mom shot back. "I hate that nickname."

"His name is *James*," Brooke replied, stepping to the side. "James Frasier Lawrence."

Mom stormed past her, slamming the door with all her might.

Brooke stood there for a long moment—okay, several long moments—trying to process everything that had just happened. She'd expected a fight about Flash. She'd considered Mom quitting as her manager a possibility, maybe.

But… Kyle Morgan was her father?

"Babe?" Flash called down softly.

Right.

"Did…" Brooke's voice broke. "Did you hear?"

Flash practically flew down the stairs to stand next to her, close enough to bump her shoulder with his. "Impossible not to."

"Yeah."

"Yeah," he agreed.

The silence stretched but it didn't feel painful. She realized Flash had laced his fingers with hers.

"I…" She cleared her throat and tried again. "I need you to stay. With me. Tonight. I…" Tears began to drip off her chin. "I don't want to be alone right now."

"You won't be."

Fifteen

"Everyone, this is Brooke Bonner, my fiancée, and our son, James Frasier," Flash announced.

Brooke cringed, although she tried not to show it. After so many months of holding her secrets close to her heart, it felt really weird to just announce Bean to four people in this room. She wasn't ready for this. She might never be ready.

But then, she'd be just as bad as her mother and she wasn't having that. So Brooke straightened her spine and lifted her chin. Really, this was no different than walking out onto a stage. Except this wasn't a stage—it was a private luxury suite in the Bridgestone Arena, where the All-Stars Rodeo would happen in a few hours. She was here to put on a show, except instead of singing her heart out, she was putting herself out there as Flash's bride-to-be.

"And this is Alex Andrews, a close friend of Brooke's," Flash went on, launching that charming grin around the room. Thank God, Alex was here. Between her oldest friend's unwavering support and Flash's dogged protectiveness, Brooke was sure she could do this.

Reasonably sure. She still had to give a convincing performance, one that had nothing to do with the last two days of Flash basically living with her, making her dinner and rocking Bean to sleep at naptime so she could lie down, too, and holding her when she cried about her mom and Kyle and the whole mess.

No, this evening had nothing to do with that glimpse into what married life could be like with Flash. It had everything to do with damage control and redemption arcs.

From a far corner, Chloe Lawrence looked up and smiled in welcome. Brooke and Flash had agreed that, for the time being, Kyle's contribution to her life was completely off-limits to anyone outside of the two of them and Alex because Brooke wasn't ready to have that part of her life implode, too.

Unfortunately, Chloe was also on the phone, so the first person Brooke got introduced to was…

"Oliver, this is Brooke," Flash said, leading Brooke over to an imposing-looking man who was clearly Flash's brother, a little taller and broader, with silver shot through his hair. Otherwise, they had practically the same eyes, the same chin. But not the same smile—that much was clear when Oliver grimaced. In an undertone, Flash added, "Be nice or *else*."

If Oliver heard the threat, he didn't react. Instead, in a deeply professional voice, he said, "Ms. Bonner, a pleasure to see you again."

Brooke notched an eyebrow at that. Flash had warned her that his brother could be a bit stiff. She'd barely met the eldest Lawrence sibling at the Fort Worth rodeo before she'd disappeared with Flash. But she remembered someone who'd been very…overwhelming, especially when compared to Flash's easygoing nature. That, at least, hadn't changed.

"Don't worry," the blonde woman next to him said, handing Oliver the baby girl she was struggling to hold on to. "The awkwardness won't last. Welcome to the Lawrence family!"

"This is Renee, Oliver's wife," Flash said, leaning over and giving Renee a kiss on the cheek. Then he mock-whispered to Brooke, "Don't believe a word she says about what we did as kids. It's lies, all lies, I say!"

Renee laughed and stuck out her hand. "I never thought I'd meet the woman who could rein Flash in, but I'm glad I finally have." Renee had a wide smile that seemed vaguely familiar. She patted the little girl. "This is our daughter, Trixie. She's almost nine months old." Trixie barely looked at Brooke before burying her head in her father's neck. "I'm so glad she has a cousin!"

Brooke exhaled in relief. Another mom, another baby—she felt less out to sea already. She only hoped Renee would prove to be as friendly as her smile.

Renee leaned forward, staring at Bean with open adoration. "Look at you," she whispered. "I know tests have to be done, but Oliver, do you see the resemblance?"

Bean chose that moment to launch one of his daddy's smiles into the room, and Renee gasped at the same time Oliver said, "Well, that settles *that*."

"Yeah," Brooke agreed. "We're all in trouble, aren't we?"

Oliver gaped and Brooke was sure she'd screwed up. But then, unexpectedly, Oliver burst out laughing. "You're going to be very good for my brother, aren't you?" he said, slugging Flash on the shoulder.

Apparently, the awkwardness didn't last long. "The better question is, how good will he be for me?"

Oliver beamed, which was sort of unsettling because when he wasn't scowling, he was almost as charming as Flash. "He better be great for you—or else."

"Boys," Renee scolded as she held out her arms. "May I?" Brooke handed over Bean, who immediately gurgled in what sounded like approval. "I practically grew up with

Flash—although he was still Frasier then. Oh, the stories I could tell you!" She fixed him with a piercing gaze. "Remember the elevator incident?"

Next to Brooke, Flash groaned. "You're killing me, Renee."

"It's good for you to be brought down a peg or two," she replied with an easy grin, and it was clear these two had a long history of teasing each other.

"I think discovering fatherhood has run me right out of pegs," Flash countered. "Come on," he said to Oliver, taking Trixie from his big brother's arms, "I could use a drink. A *ginger ale*," he said, meeting Oliver's scowl head-on. "Sheesh, man. Even when I drank, I never drank before a rodeo. Babe, you want green tea? I had them get some just for you."

Brooke's cheeks heated. "That would be wonderful. Thank you."

Flash winked at her, and then the brothers headed off to the side of the suite where a variety of nonalcoholic beverages were displayed on a sideboard.

"I remember when Trixie was this little," Renee said, bouncing Bean in her arms. The baby trilled in delight. She eyed Brooke sympathetically. "How are you holding up?"

"Okay, I guess." Sure, she hadn't seen or spoken to her mother in two days, nor had she decided what to do about Kyle Morgan.

At least Alex was here. Brooke glanced over to see that Flash had somehow gotten Alex over to the drinks and was introducing her to Trixie. It was sweet of Flash to make sure Alex was a part of what was, essentially, a family gathering. And despite all her protestations that she wasn't going to like Flash, Brooke could tell her friend was relieved Flash was including her.

"I understand Chloe has a whole plan in place," Renee said.

Brooke felt awkward standing in the middle of the room,

so she moved to the huge picture windows that overlooked the arena. Renee followed. Below, she saw someone who might be Pete Wellington making the final preparations. In a few minutes, the doors would open and the stands would begin to fill. And once the crowd was in place...

It was just another performance, one where she wouldn't have a guitar in her hands. Just a baby. "Yes. I ran it through the record label's PR department and they signed off on it, as well. I think Chloe's got a job at the label if she ever gets tired of the rodeo."

"Trust me, that'll never happen. The only one who's tired of the rodeo is Oliver."

Redemption arcs for everyone, apparently. Chloe was probably on the phone with Kari right now, coordinating the Big Reveal, as Brooke had started to think of it.

Right before Flash's first event, she and Bean, who had his own set of baby-sized noise-canceling headphones, would go behind the chutes where she would very publicly give Flash a kiss for good luck. The cameras would zoom in to capture the moment. Alex would be right behind her, just in case.

The announcers would draw everyone's attention to her and Flash, at which point Flash would lift Bean out of Brooke's arms and cuddle him. If Bean was cooperative, he would smile, and Brooke would put her head on Flash's shoulder and it would be perfect.

Brooke looked at her son, who was currently attempting to stuff his whole fist in his drooly mouth. Life was so rarely perfect. "It's going to be very messy for a while, though," she said, and sighed.

To Brooke's surprise, Renee wrapped an arm around her shoulders and gave Brooke an awkward hug. "You'll get through this," she said. "No matter what happens, you and this special little guy are family now and family is everything to the Lawrences."

"It is?" Brooke was horrified to hear her voice catch. Family had done nothing but let her down for the last few days. Weeks. Lifetimes, it seemed.

Renee nodded. "It absolutely is. Even when Flash had a rough few years there—which he mostly brought upon himself," she quickly added, "his family stood by him. I don't know your history, aside from your official bio. But my own family was—" she shrugged and turned her attention to Bean "—less than ideal. Having the Lawrences stand with me when everyone else bailed? It's *everything*."

Brooke blinked hard. "I don't really have anyone else but Alex. My mother stopped speaking to me when she found out about Flash." That was a gross simplification of the situation, but it was all she could cop to without crying.

At least with Flash in the house, she'd been able to get some more sleep. She wouldn't have had a prayer of getting through this night otherwise.

Renee handed Bean back to Brooke and then gave her another sideways hug. "I'll be honest—the Lawrences can be overbearing, overwhelming and completely over-the-top. But they'll fight for you and this little guy until the very end, if you let them."

Bean launched his daddy's smile at Brooke. "I just want things to work out," she said softly, hugging her baby tight.

"They will," Renee promised. "Just maybe not the way you thought they would."

Flash stood off to the side, making Trixie giggle as he blew bubbles on her tummy. The whole time, he watched Brooke, who was deep in conversation with Renee.

Chloe came up and topped off her water. "It seems to be going well," she said, nodding toward the two women.

Flash introduced Chloe to Alex. "She's nervous," Alex announced. "Excuse me."

"I'd be worried if she weren't," Chloe agreed. Once Alex had joined Renee and Brooke, Chloe turned her full attention to Flash. "All the pieces are in place. You know what you need to do, right?"

"Yes. I knew the last three times you asked, too."

He was not going to let everyone's nervousness get to him, though. The situation was under control. The babies were happy, the tea was steeping and Brooke's introduction to his family was going well. Really, really well.

He still couldn't get over the fight between Brooke and her mother, though. Meeting Crissy Bonner had made sense of a lot of stuff. He could see how Brooke had been completely overruled by her mother, how Brooke keeping Flash's contribution to their son quiet hadn't necessarily been a selfish act but one of quiet rebellion.

Oh, he was still plenty mad at Crissy Bonner. But between that fight and everything Brooke had told him since then, it was getting a lot harder to hold on to his anger at Brooke herself. He'd always understood on a logical level that she hadn't told him about the baby because she'd seen those headlines and panicked. But when he counted how Brooke's mom had been manipulating her...

Brooke had stood up for Flash. More than that, she'd stood up for herself.

God, she was amazing. And, better than that, she was wearing his ring.

Oliver rumbled, "You *are* going to marry her, aren't you?" while snatching Trixie from Flash's arms.

"That is the literal definition of *engaged*," Flash said, refusing to allow any resentment to take hold at the note of doubt in Oliver's voice. "But I'm not going to drag her down the aisle tomorrow. That was the deal."

"Of course I'm not saying that." This serious declaration was interrupted by Oliver spinning in a circle with his daughter, making the baby shriek with glee. "I'm saying, make it legal."

"Working on it," Flash said through gritted teeth as he squeezed the honey into Brooke's tea.

Chloe slapped Oliver on the arm. "It's been four days, dude. Give the man some room to work. We have a plan." She turned back to Flash. Any gratitude he might have felt toward her for standing up for him evaporated when she added, "You remember your part, right?"

"Would you two back off?" Flash was really proud of the way he kept his voice calm. "I'm not going to blow up and I'm not going to lash out. I know why I'm here and what I'm supposed to do, so stop acting like I'm still nineteen, got it?"

Chloe and Oliver exchanged a look. It did not inspire a great deal of confidence.

"Got it?" Flash said more forcefully.

His phone buzzed—a message from Dad. Good luck tonight—and bring that girl and that baby home on Monday! I want to meet my grandson!

Flash grinned. At least they'd convinced Dad to stay home for this night. Things tended to go haywire when he showed up at rodeos. Besides, Flash hadn't wanted to overwhelm Brooke with relatives and if Milt Lawrence was anything, it was overwhelming.

Will do. Thanks, Dad, he texted back.

"You need to head down," Chloe said after listening to the earpiece. Pete was no doubt on the other end. "Hey— about the Cowboy of the Year championship…"

"Listen," he told his siblings. "I'm still in it to win it, okay? Tomorrow we'll work on setting up visitation schedules around the All-Stars and her concert dates. But that's tomorrow. Tonight, I'm counting on you to keep Brooke and James safe and happy. Do *not* upset her. No mentioning lawyers or money or anything that starts with the phrase 'you should.' Can you handle that?"

"Of course," Oliver scoffed, as if he hadn't spent a few decades telling Flash what he should or should not be doing.

"Promise," Chloe added, looking about as chastised as Flash had ever seen her. "The situation is under control."

"The more you say that, the more worried I get," Flash muttered as he cut around them and headed toward Brooke, tea in hand.

Awkward family meetings aside, this was the sort of thing he could get used to. Brooke and James were looking out at the arena. They'd watch him ride and then they'd head back to her place for the night. James would probably exercise his lungs at some point in the wee hours and Flash would get up with him, letting Brooke sleep as long as possible. Then they'd flop back in bed together, taking comfort in each other's bodies.

He hadn't been lying—tomorrow would bring schedules and negotiations and complications. But tonight was his. This was his rodeo and she was…

She might just be his forever.

Because if he married her, there was no going back on that. Lawrence men—and women—were one-and-done people.

"Hey, I've got to head down," he said, slipping his arm around her waist and pulling her back against his chest. Renee shot him a wink and excused herself. Alex did the same, giving him and Brooke as much privacy as possible in the crowded suite. "Your tea. Doing okay?"

"Your sister-in-law is nice," she said, and he was thankful to hear relief in her voice. "I didn't tell her everything, but I got the feeling she'd understand."

"She would. She's one of the nicest people I've ever known, but—and I mean this—don't ever trust her when she's holding water balloons."

Brooke chuckled, which made Bean look up from where he was gumming a rattle.

"You up for this, little man?" Flash asked, stroking his son's soft hair. A week ago, he'd been a single man, pining for the woman of his dreams. Now?

Now he was so much more.

James grinned around his rattle.

"That's my boy." Flash leaned his chin onto Brooke's shoulder. "We're going to get through this, babe. Just a few hours and then we'll be back home. You can do it."

She blew a hard breath. "Trust me, no one knows that the show must go on like I do. Now get going."

"I'm going—but I'm coming back," he said with a grin, kissing her on the neck. "See you soon." When he turned around, he found the attention of every single person in the room on him. Oliver almost smiled, which was the same as a normal person jumping for joy. Chloe gave Flash a thumbs-up, and he could tell that was exactly the sort of display she wanted to see in an hour. Renee beamed a huge smile at him, and even Alex nodded in approval.

So far, so good. Now they just had to get through the rodeo without tanking his place in the standings, and then he could have Brooke all to himself again.

Yup, he was feeling lucky tonight.

Sixteen

"Ready?" Alex muttered.

"Yes."

This was just ten minutes out of Brooke's life. She'd basically handed over the reins of her social media to Chloe and Kari so she wouldn't have to deal with the notifications for a few days. So really, this was no big deal.

Brooke did a final check on Bean's headphones to make sure the baby hadn't knocked them off in the last three minutes. Then she squared her shoulders and put her game face on.

"And Dan Jones makes the time!" an announcer yelled over the roar of the crowd.

Dan was their cue.

"It's time," Chloe said, guiding them out from the tiny alcove created underneath the chutes that had been blocked off from public view by promotional banners. Brooke followed and Alex brought up the rear.

They climbed the rickety metal stairs to the top of the chutes where Flash was waiting. He turned to her just as the announcer said, "Up next is Flash Lawrence, who's having a heck of a comeback year."

"Hey babe," Flash said over the roar of the crowd as he stepped into her. "You okay?"

She knew it was for the show, that they were both playing to the cameras; still, the obvious concern in his eyes was touching. "Holding steady," she said as he lowered her head to hers.

"Good girl," he murmured against her lips.

"That's right," the other announcer said. "After a rough...uh, Jimbo? Who's Flash kissing?"

Brooke kept her eyes closed because she didn't really want to see Flash kissing her blown up on a jumbotron.

"Is that Nashville's own Brooke Bonner, the country superstar?" Jimbo asked. "Larry, is there something going on we didn't know about?"

A hush fell over the arena, and Brooke knew everyone was staring and asking the same questions.

"Almost there," Flash whispered as he lifted Bean out of her arms. "Being good for Mommy?" he asked as he pressed a kiss to the one small section of Bean's head the headphones weren't covering. And, bless his little heart, Bean smiled.

Brooke exhaled in relief and remembered to smile. Hopefully, it looked real and not like she was having a low-grade panic attack, because there was no going back now. Bean was officially public knowledge.

"Jimbo—is that a *baby*? Did you know Flash Lawrence had a baby?"

The crowd gasped in complete unison as Brooke flattened her palm high on Flash's chest so the massive diamond he'd bought her was right next to Bean's back.

"Larry, is that an *engagement* ring?" Jimbo asked.

"Look at the size of that rock!" Larry was clearly impressed.

Seconds later, the crowd erupted into cheers so deafening that even with his protective headphones, Bean flinched.

"Flash, you're up!" Pete said. "Good job, everyone!"

Brooke took Bean back and gave Flash a kiss for luck while the crowd cheered. So far, so good. She'd been in front of enough audiences to know they had the arena eating out of the palms of their hands. This might be a show, but it was a good one.

And Flash knew it.

"Proud of you, Brooke," he said, his satisfied smile almost enough to make her forget they were being watched by thousands.

"Jimbo, I bet there's more to this story—I hope we'll be able to get a word with Flash after the show?" Larry asked.

"Boy, me too," Jimbo agreed. "But first, he's got to make the time on this bronco!" Thankfully, they turned the conversation back to the horse's stats.

"Have a good ride," she told him, digging deep for that smile.

With a nod, he turned and climbed down into the chute onto the bronco's back. Brooke edged away from the chute so Pete could help Flash get his ropes adjusted.

"Damn near perfect," Alex muttered behind Brooke.

She nodded but didn't look away from Flash. The gate opened and his horse spun out, bucking high into the air while Flash held on for dear life.

"That's Daddy, sweetie," she murmured to Bean, shifting the baby so he could watch. "Look at him go!"

Seconds ticked by slowly as Flash clung to the horse's back. The buzzer sounded just as Flash lost his fight with gravity and he went tumbling to the dirt. Brooke gasped and held her breath, but Flash popped right back up again, pumping his fist into the air.

"Looks like it's Flash's lucky night," Jimbo said. "That ride's going to earn him first in the rankings!"

Brooke cheered along with the crowd. She'd almost made it. Now she just had to wait for Flash to get back to the chute, and then he'd escort her backstage, where he'd hand her off to Chloe, who'd take her back to the family's suite for the rest of the rodeo.

"Well, well, well—this explains everything, doesn't it?" a silky voice said, cutting through the crowd noise and the announcers.

Brooke spun just as Alex snarled, "Hey, back off."

The cowboy staring at Brooke wasn't wearing a vest or a rider's number, but he looked vaguely familiar. Had she met him before? Or just seen his picture somewhere?

"Easy, honey," the cowboy said to Alex, which made the big woman growl. "I'm an...old friend of Flash's." He gave Brooke the once-over, and a burst of apprehension shot down her back.

"Explains what?" she asked, looking around for Pete or Chloe or *anyone*. She did not like the look in this guy's eyes.

"He was screwing you the entire time. How about that?" The cowboy laughed but when Alex went to shove him back, he spun gracefully past her, and suddenly only a foot separated Brooke from him.

Oh, hell. She couldn't back up because there was no room and she couldn't get to the stairs without getting past him. "Leave us alone," she ordered.

"Hey!" Flash shouted from the arena floor. How close was he? Where was Pete? Why couldn't Alex catch this guy? "Tex, back off! Pete! Alex! Get him away from her!"

"You know your little boy toy beat the ever-loving shit out of me?" the cowboy apparently named Tex all but purred. Another hush fell over the arena, but Brooke could feel the difference between this one and the way the crowd had quieted at the reveal of the baby and the ring. "Broke my jaw and my leg, all because I hoped you'd be a good fuck. He ended my career, all for a little piece like you!"

Behind Tex, Alex lunged but the man had catlike reflexes, apparently, because he easily danced out of her way—which only brought him closer to Brooke.

"I had nothing to do with that," she told him, curling around Bean. That's why she recognized him—his picture had been in the articles about Flash's arrest and trial. Had the fight been about her? Because this creep made some creepy comments?

Someone in the crowd shrieked. "Larry, what's Tex McGraw doing here?" Jimbo asked.

"He quit the All-Stars, didn't he?" Larry responded, sounding worried. "After that fight with Flash?"

"The bastard took away everything I love," Tex said, charging forward, his hand clamping around her arm with so much force that it took her breath away. "It's time I returned the favor."

Brooke tried to yell, but her throat wasn't working as Tex twisted her arm hard enough that she saw stars. The baby! She spun, trying to keep hold of Bean, who began to scream bloody murder.

"Brooke!" A body slammed into Tex—oh, thank God, it was Flash.

Brooke stumbled before Tex's grip on her arm gave, and then Flash and Tex crashed off the top of the chute, landing in the dirt with a thud. Flash came up swinging.

"Jesus," Alex said, grabbing Brooke and hustling her down the stairs. "Is Bean okay?"

Brooke stumbled to a stop, staring in horror as Flash threw a punch and then another one. His fists were a blur. "You touch her again and I'll *end* you," he roared as blood flew off his knuckles.

"Move, Bonner," Alex bellowed, shoving Brooke past the fight and into the tunnel under the stands. *"Move!"*

Brooke looked back over her shoulder as Alex pushed her away from the arena. Complete pandemonium had broken out—Pete and a bunch of cowboys were trying to get Flash off Tex, who was throwing a few punches of his own.

The last thing Brooke saw before Alex dragged her through a pair of doors was Flash's head snap back as Tex's fist connected with his jaw and Flash turning a bloody grin on Tex, letting his fist fly.

Brooke's stomach turned and she began to run.

God help her, that man was enjoying the fight.

Seventeen

"The *good* news," Chloe said in the tone of voice that made it clear there wasn't a whole lot to go around, "is that, despite your record and your history with Tex, the prosecutors are declining to press charges on assault for you. The whole fight was caught on camera. You were clearly defending your family. Oliver's talking to them now."

That was the good news? Flash moved the ice off his face and squinted at Chloe. "The bad news?"

Wincing at his black eyes, Chloe held her phone out for Flash to read. Which was a challenge. The words drifted before him like they were floating down a lazy river, but he managed to get one eye to focus.

What he saw chilled him colder than any ice pack ever could. Brooke had sent a group text to Chloe, Oliver and Flash: Thank you for welcoming me and James into the Lawrence family. We will be in touch to set up a visitation schedule. No mention of Flash coming back to her house tonight, no mention of engagements—nothing.

His vision narrowed to those few lines of text. He forgot how to count, how to breathe.

We will be in touch.

If it were possible for five words to break him, those five might just do the trick.

She'd promised. *Promised!* They were in this together now! They were a team! She'd sworn she wouldn't keep him from his son—not again!

No. He refused to accept this.

He had to make this right. He struggled up, which made the room spin. "I need to go," he said, except his jaw wasn't moving right—again. If people could stop breaking the damn thing, that'd be great. He couldn't talk to Brooke with a broken jaw and he definitely couldn't ride.

"No," Pete said, putting a firm hand on Flash's shoulder, "you don't. You show up looking like someone flattened your face with a steamroller and it'll only scare her more."

"Worse than the cushion incident in the library," Chloe agreed, picking up the ice and putting it back on Flash's face.

He tried to bat it away because, yeah, he probably looked horrifying, but he couldn't let Brooke hide behind that cold text. "Tomorrow, then," he managed to get out.

"Shit, man—is your jaw busted again?" Pete said, crouching before Flash and studying his face.

"You should see the other guy," Flash tried to say but that was way too much talking. Crap.

"Buddy, you're done for the season," Pete said. "Chloe, we've got to get him to a hospital."

"On it," she said, and sighed.

His championship season…gone. Just like that.

But the moment self-pity tried to crowd into his head, it was pushed aside by the look of terror on Brooke's face when Tex had grabbed her. In that moment, she'd been more important than anything else—his jaw, the rodeo… none of it mattered. What had mattered was making sure she was okay and Bean was safe.

He couldn't wait until tomorrow.

He needed to see with his own eyes that she was fine, that the baby was okay, that Brooke understood he'd do anything to protect her.

We will be in touch.

He needed her to have some faith in him. Instead, she was pulling back, locking him out.

He wasn't going to stand for it.

"I will knock your ass out if you try to stand up again," Pete warned, shoving him back into the chair. "I've done it before and I'll do it again."

The room spun. Flash might have blacked out, he wasn't sure. Maybe Pete really had tagged him. The next thing he knew, he was being loaded into the back of an ambulance and Oliver was next to him, looking as worried as hell.

"It's going to be okay," Oliver said, his voice sounding strained.

"Brooke," Flash moaned. The ambulance began to move and the world got spinny again.

"It'll be okay," Oliver repeated, holding on to Flash's arm.

As Flash slipped back into the darkness, he was pretty sure it wouldn't be okay. Not until he could get to Brooke.

Thankfully, Bean was fine. Once Brooke settled in the rocker with the baby on her lap, he was out like a light.

Brooke, however, was not fine.

She had forgotten what *fine* felt like. Every one of her nightmares had played out in real time—Flash Lawrence, out of control.

"You're still shaking," Alex said, sounding as close to crying as Brooke had ever heard her.

"Am I?" Brooke laughed, a high-pitched noise that startled Bean. Brooke adjusted him to the other side. "Sorry."

"I sent that text you wanted," Alex said, sitting down on the footstool.

"What text?"

The worry lines deepened on Alex's face. She pulled out a phone—Brooke's phone, she recognized it—and read the text. "You told me to send it when we got home, so I did."

"Then I must have wanted you to." She didn't remember telling Alex that, but who knew. She was pretty sure she was in a state of shock.

She'd been nearly assaulted and then her fiancé had snapped, and none of that took into account the situation with her mother and Kyle or the press...

It was safe to say she was *not* coping well. Nope.

"Brooke? If he shows up, do you want to see him?"

"I don't..." She cleared her throat. A part of her wished that Flash would stroll into the nursery, a mug of hot tea with honey in his hand and a charming smile on his face. That he'd bring the music back with him and they'd write the ending to their song together.

But how could she trust him? How could she trust that she'd make the right decision this time?

Thank God she hadn't married him.

She held up her left hand, where his enormous ring was heavy on her finger. It hadn't been real. That was a comfort, right? No one would blame her for breaking it off with him, not after what had happened tonight.

"I don't think so," she said softly.

"Are you sure that's the right thing to do?" Alex asked, her voice gruff.

"I thought you didn't like him."

"I don't. But Brooke, he was defending you. Because I missed." Tears overflowed Alex's eyes. Brooke stared in shock. Had Alex ever cried? "I wasn't quick enough to catch that guy, but Flash was faster. If I'd done my job..." A sob racked her big body. "I'm so sorry I let you down. But don't hold it against Flash. He was *protecting* you."

Was Alex right? After all, hadn't Brooke been up there

on that chute, praying he'd get to her in time? And he had. He had!

Someone rang the damned doorbell and Bean startled, mewling in displeasure.

"I'll get it," Alex growled, rubbing at her watery eyes.

Sighing, Brooke began to pat the baby's back. "If it's Flash, I'm not home." Maybe Alex was right, maybe she wasn't. But Brooke wasn't going to deal with any of that tonight. No way, no how.

Being around Flash was too intoxicating. He made her forget things, like how Bean was her first priority and how she didn't need someone who was good in bed—she could go whole years without sex. She had after she'd met him, hadn't she? But the moment he got within ten feet of her, she craved him like a junkie craved a hit.

That wasn't healthy.

Two sets of footsteps echoed on the stairs. Oh, no—Alex had decided to let Flash in after all, hadn't she? "I told you, I didn't want to see…"

But it wasn't Flash who followed Alex into the room—it was Kyle Morgan. Of course. Because Brooke didn't have enough going on today.

"What do you want?"

Kyle had the decency to look embarrassed. "Caught the rodeo on TV tonight."

"So? What do you care?"

Kyle blushed. "Didn't know you'd had a baby. Sorry I missed that."

"Are you?" She knew she was being a total witch, but she couldn't help it. Anyone who was expecting her to go along to get along was in for a hell of a surprise. "Are you my father?"

Kyle dropped his gaze, scrubbing his hand through his short silver hair. "She finally told you, huh?"

"I will never let you see your grandson ever again if

you don't cut the crap, Morgan. I've had a shitty evening and you're not helping. You've been my friend for years and never once even hinted that you were my damned father, so *spill it.*"

"Look, I got your mother pregnant. We had a couple of wild nights and…"

Alex growled menacingly behind him.

"And I didn't want to be a father. I was too young and I'll be honest—I was doing a lot of drugs. I wasn't fit to be around a baby. Told your mother as much. Told her I wasn't going to be a father to any child she had. She made the choice to keep you."

"Oh. Okay. So you really didn't want me. Sure."

If this night got any worse, Brooke was going to lose her mind. She couldn't take another shock.

"Morgan, that's the crappiest excuse I've ever heard," Alex rumbled.

"Yeah, I know," he shot back, but he kept his attention on Brooke. "By the time you were a kid, I'd gotten clean and my songs started selling and you had so much talent…" He cleared his throat. "I'm not father material. Never was. But a mentor? I could do that. Your mother saw the same thing I did—you had what it took to be a star. And I could help make it happen."

Brooke let her head fall back against the chair. This man was her father. And in his screwed-up way, he'd done his part to look after her. It hadn't been enough, but it'd been something.

"Look, I may have messed up," Kyle began.

"You think?" Brooke shot back.

"But I did the best I could. I didn't have anything else to give, especially before I stopped using. It's been the joy of my life, being a part of your music." He stared at Bean. "Wish your mother had told me you were going to have a baby, though. Sorry I missed that," he repeated.

Brooke couldn't look at him. She closed her eyes and her mind immediately turned to Flash. What would he do, if he were here? Would he throw Kyle out on his rear? Get into another fight? Or would he stand next to Brooke, holding her hand and ready to back her up, no matter what she decided?

Kyle had had a fling with Crissy Bonner and left her high and dry. When he'd found out about Brooke, he'd cut and run.

Flash hadn't done that, though.

Instead, he'd offered her and Bean the protection of his name and his family's power and wealth. He'd done it in a crappy way at first, but one thing had been clear from the very moment he'd found out about Bean—he'd move heaven and earth to be a father to his son.

Was that still true?

"Why is my name Bonner?"

"Morgan is a stage name." She cracked open one eye to glare at him. "What? I had a lot of kids calling me Bonnie when I was growing up. I married your mother to give you a name and then we got a quiet, quick divorce."

Of all the damn things…insisting that he give her his real name but not anything else took the cake. "I am going to hate you for a while." Which was a lie. She was going to hate him for as long as she damn well wanted. And she wasn't going to think too kindly about Mom, either. The level of deception they'd sunk to was mind-boggling. And for what?

She was so tired of lies wrapped in lies and buried under more lies.

Kyle looked hurt but he nodded grimly. "That's fine." He stood to leave. "I've always cared about you, honey. That doesn't mean I haven't been the world's worst father," he said over the combined sounds of Brooke and Alex scoffing in unison, "but I still care. If you let me, I'll care about that boy of yours, too."

"Don't push your luck, *Kyle*." Because she wasn't calling him Dad. He definitely hadn't earned that right.

He nodded in resignation again and turned to go. "One last thing—that fiancé of yours?"

"I don't think we're engaged anymore," Brooke mumbled.

"Yeah, I looked him up after the Bluebird. Those headlines must have pissed your mother off in a major way—too close to what happened to her and me, I think."

Brooke scowled at him again. "You got a point? I've had a long night and I want James to get some sleep." She might not get any, but someone in this house should.

"James. Good name. Fits him." He leaned forward and Brooke let him brush a kiss against her forehead. "I walked away from you and your mother. It's always been my biggest regret, that I threw away the love of my life and my family just because it got hard. Don't make the same mistakes I did."

"That supposed to be fatherly advice?" she snipped, because it was either be snippy or start bawling.

Kyle gave her a sad smile as he turned to go. "Just… think about it. Let me know when you want to talk." He straightened. "I'm not going to throw away a second chance to be a part of your life. You have always been my greatest hit, honey."

Alex showed him out, leaving Brooke alone with her tumbled thoughts and her sleeping son. Now that some of the shock of the attack and fight was wearing off, she was more confused than ever.

Kyle Morgan was her father, but he'd completely abdicated any responsibility for her, choosing to be a friend instead of a parent. He'd abandoned Mom, but had helped Brooke as she'd worked her way up in country music. But he hadn't wanted her unless she was easy and talented. He was a selfish, egotistical asshole, and forgiveness would be a long time coming, if ever.

Flash, on the other hand, wanted to marry her and make it legal—not just in name only, like Kyle and Crissy had, but as a real family. He wanted to be a part of Bean's life. He'd talked about building her a studio on his ranch in Texas and buying Bean a pony. He'd introduced her to his family and staked his claim in front of what felt like the whole world.

Was what happened tonight a deal breaker? Or was she overreacting? If she walked away from Flash, was she doing the same thing Kyle had done? Pushing Flash out of her life because it was easier?

She simply didn't know what the right answer was.

Probably because there wasn't one.

Eighteen

Flash woke up in the hospital to find Milt Lawrence sitting next to the bed, watching baseball. That seemed off. Dad was supposed to be in Texas. Texas was a long way from Nashville. Or was Flash in Texas?

"What time is it?" Flash asked groggily. Or tried to. Damn it, his jaw had been wired shut again.

"High time you woke up," Dad replied, clicking off the television. "That was a hell of a concussion that ass gave you. But don't worry," he went on, and Flash thought the old man winked, but it was hard to tell because one of Flash's eyes was swollen. "You did a hell of a lot more damage."

That sounded bad. "Didn't kill him?"

"Naw, he's alive and pissed. You've bested him twice. His pride is never going to recover and Oliver's working to have him brought up on charges. Plus, your sister has banned him from ever entering an All-Stars event again and I believe she's gotten him kicked off the Total Bull Challenge, too. She can be very persuasive when she wants to be." Dad chuckled. "Mighty proud of that girl, going to the mat for her family like that."

Flash grunted.

Dad stood on bow legs and peered down at Flash's face. It took Flash's eyes a second to focus. "Never known anyone who had such a glass jaw but could keep fighting."

"Thanks, Dad," he slurred. He didn't care about his jaw at the moment. He only cared about two things. "Brooke? Baby?"

Dad's smile cracked a little and he sat back down. "They're fine. Not really in the mood to deal with your brother and sister. That friend of hers has been sending updates, though."

Flash tried to think, but he could tell he was on painkillers. His brain was muddy and he couldn't see through the silt. Dad couldn't be saying what Flash was afraid he was saying. "Need her."

"Not sure that's the best idea at the moment," Dad said, sounding sad about it. "You gave her quite a fright. But, hell, I saw the tape. I'd have done the exact same thing. When someone threatens the woman you love, you step up and throw down to protect her. You did the right thing."

"Don't *love* her." Funny, those words really hurt to say.

Thankfully, Dad was having no trouble understanding Flash's slurring. "That's not what it looked like to me, boy."

"Like her. Lots." Protecting her had been the most important thing he'd ever done and, if he had to, he'd beat the hell out of Tex again. Anything to take care of her and James. "Need her."

"Son," Dad began in that tone that signaled Flash was in for a hell of a lecture, "I don't know who you think you're trying to fool, but I've got eyes and I've loved my Trixie far longer than you've been walking on this planet."

"She doesn't trust me," Flash said, or tried to say. "She hid the baby from me."

"So?"

Flash managed to roll his eyes at that, although it hurt like hell.

"I'm serious," Dad said, leaning forward to meet Flash's gaze. "No, I don't think she should've kept that kid from you—but I can count, son. I did the math. I'm betting she saw those headlines, just like everyone else did. And your sister says that Brooke's mother is a problem."

"Huge problem," Flash agreed. His father was making sense. Never a good sign.

"So she had her reasons. And you have yours. But if you're waiting for the stars to line up and everything to be perfect in a relationship, then you're gonna spend the rest of your life alone, pining for the girl that got away from you. You're in love with her, and don't even try to deny it—I *know* you, boy. She's pretty crazy for you, too, from what I can tell. But everything that comes after that, including faith and trust and love, is a choice. Every day you have to choose to do what it takes to be in love, to stay in love and then? Then you've got to do the work."

Flash blinked at his old man in confusion. "But…you and Mom?"

Milt Lawrence snorted. "There were times your mother, bless her soul, didn't like me very much. More than once she almost strung me up by my toes and I'm not too proud to admit I deserved it. And, as much as it pains me to say, there were days when she drove me up a wall. We had our fights, although we made sure you kids didn't know. But the next day, we'd choose to love each other all over again and *do the work*. Every single day, I made it my job to show her not just that I loved her and needed her and trusted her, but that I was the man she could love, trust and need, come hell or high water." He snorted again. "I never cheated. I made time for her. I put her needs first and I was there for you kids. And let me tell you, flowers never hurt a thing."

Was Flash hearing this right? His parents' marriage had always seemed so perfect—a love story for the ages. At no point had it looked like *work*.

"A year ago…" Dad rubbed his chin thoughtfully. "A year ago, I don't think you would've been capable of it. I sure as hell wouldn't have told you to go get your girl. Wouldn't have been fair to the girl," he added with a chuckle.

"Thanks, Dad," Flash slurred. His head was spinning and he had no idea if it was the drugs or the concussion or the jaw or…

The truth.

He and Brooke hadn't chosen each other after their one-night stand. But doing the work…that sounded a lot like proving Brooke could trust him.

Would she choose to prove he could trust her? Or would she bail?

Dad kept going. "But you got your act together. You did the work on yourself and, Lord knows, I've never been prouder of you. So now? Now I know you can do the right thing. I know you've got it in you, Flash."

A warm feeling spread through Flash's chest. He had, hadn't he? That year of sobriety and anger management and, yes, celibacy had been the longest, hardest year of his life. Every single day he'd had to get up and choose to stay on the straight and narrow, even when it sucked.

There wasn't just one thing he could do or say that would prove to Brooke he was worthy of her. He had to show her, day in and day out. It'd take a lifetime to prove it, but it'd be a lifetime with her.

Because he loved her.

Damn it, he hated when his dad was right. Made the man insufferable.

"So give her a few days to cool off. You don't have a choice—you're being held for observation for that concussion." He sighed heavily. "Flash, you're not gonna want to hear this, but…"

For a panicked second, Flash thought Brooke had called

in lawyers. But then Dad wouldn't be giving him that pep talk if Brooke was done with him, right?

"Your jaw can't take another break," Dad said, his voice...sad, almost. "This one is going to take a few more surgeries before it's all said and done." He cleared his throat, a sound like a tractor engine turning over. "Might not be best for you to compete anymore."

That sounded like... *the end*. The end of a career.

Like his body couldn't take the jarring from bucking broncos and bulls, like steer wrestling was completely off the table. Maybe he could still do calf roping?

Oh, hell—was he done? *Done* done?

No.

No! This was his year! Cowboy of the Year was his for the taking! He'd finally earned his place at the table and he was the best in the world! Hell, he'd been chasing the rodeo for over half his life. If he wasn't chasing the buckle, what was he doing?

But the moment the question crossed his fuzzy mind, the answer followed it. He'd known it since he'd seen Brooke up there, trying to protect their son from Tex.

Nothing mattered more than she did.

Brooke and Bean were everything to him. The rodeo was...just a job.

He'd be a husband and a father. He'd be there to read bedtime stories to his son and travel with Brooke when she toured. Maybe there'd be more children, babies he'd be able to hold the moment they came into the world. Brooke would test her songs out for him, and he'd be by her side when she did things like walk the red carpet at the Grammys or the Country Music Awards.

A family of love and laughter, for the rest of his life. That was his future. Not another buckle or another brawl.

Or another broken jaw.

He'd show up and do the work because Brooke was worth it.

One problem with that plan.

He needed to get to Brooke right *now*.

Dad grabbed his hand away from the IV before Flash could pull it out. "Knock that off, son. You're no good to anyone all busted up."

"How long?" He had hazy memories of time passing, but clearly he'd been sedated so the doctors could work on his jaw. Stupid head injuries.

"Day and a half. Oliver sent the company jet to get me." His phone chimed. "Hey, listen to this—your sister forwarded this to me. Know what the press is saying? Here. 'Flash Lawrence Defends Fiancée Brooke Bonner in All-Stars Brawl.' You're a hero, son."

Yeah, a hero to everyone. Did that include Brooke?

"Need her," he mumbled to his father.

"I know you do. Lawrence men fall hard and fast and forever. It was the same with your mother, God rest her soul."

A hush settled in the hospital room, except for all the beeping. Hey, he'd noticed the beeping! Maybe his head was starting to clear.

Then it came to him. Flowers were great, but he needed to show Brooke that he knew her and cared for her.

"Tea," Flash managed to say. Yeah, his head was definitely clearing because his jaw was starting to throb. But the pain was good. It centered him and gave him something to fight against.

"What was that?" Dad leaned in closer.

"Send her tea. And honey. Good honey. From me."

Dad leaned into Flash's line of sight, a crafty grin on his face. "That," he said, "I can do."

Nineteen

"Just so we're all operating on the same page, let's look at the footage," Kari Stockard, the PR exec, said as the footage of the All-Stars Rodeo from two weeks ago began to run. "As you can see, we arranged for Brooke and the baby to be behind the chutes for a touching moment with Flash Lawrence."

Two weeks since Brooke had last seen Flash. It felt like a lifetime. She kept telling herself she was still making up her mind about him, but that was a lie.

She was doing the exact same thing she'd done after she'd discovered she was pregnant. She was hiding.

And she hated it.

Brooke stared in horrified fascination as her life played out on the screen in a conference room at her record label's executive offices, surrounded by men in suits and her new manager, Janet Worthington. Bean trilled in delight when the camera zoomed in on Brooke's face. Because Bean went everywhere with her now. She didn't have to hide him anymore. And also, because Mom was no longer his primary babysitter.

She didn't want to watch the exact moment she'd lost

control of her life again. She was still having nightmares about living it.

But she was seeing it now while Kari talked over the video. Brooke watched as Flash kissed her and then cuddled Bean, and it took Brooke's breath away because it'd all been for show, right?

But that's not what she saw. What she saw was *real*. Real adoration in Flash's eyes when he'd looked at her, real tenderness as he'd held his son.

She saw real love in her eyes when she'd kissed him for good luck.

It was as plain as day that Flash Lawrence loved her.

It was all over his face, in every single movement he made, in every touch between them. He was head over heels in love with her. And she…

The camera caught her touching her lips as Flash walked away from her, a happy smile lighting up her face. She didn't even remember doing that, but apparently she had.

Oh, God—it hadn't been for show.

It'd been real. All of it.

The camera cut back to Brooke and Bean, still on top of the chute. This time, that terrible Tex McGraw started advancing on her.

Brooke gasped in shock to see the horror that'd been on her face. She watched helplessly as Alex lunged but missed and suddenly Tex had hold of Brooke, his hand digging into her arm and then…

Then Flash had been there, moving so fast he was little more than a blur. He'd gotten Tex off her and she had to swallow back tears as she watched herself stumble, struggling to hold on to her son. Then Alex rushed her down from the chutes, and that was when the video clicked off and a graph came up on the screen.

Kari was talking again but Brooke couldn't listen. She had to keep her gaze on the top of Bean's head while she struggled for control. The incident was every bit as bad as she remembered and yet…not as bad, either.

Because Flash loved her. It was *so* obvious.

Why hadn't she seen it at the time?

What would Tex McGraw have done if Flash hadn't been there?

Alex had been right. Brooke hadn't been able to separate her terror at the attack from her feelings for Flash. All those emotions had sloshed around, mixing together.

She looked down at Flash's ring glinting brightly on her finger.

It'd been real to Flash. She remembered him saying he wouldn't ask her to marry him again, but the offer was on the table. She'd thought he'd been asking her out of duty or a concern about custody.

But had he really been asking her to marry him?

"As you can see from this chart, the number of social media hits from the last two weeks has been tremendous and the reception has been overwhelmingly positive," Kari explained to the bored-looking suits. "People are not only excited for Brooke's new album, but they can't get enough of Brooke and Flash!"

He had. He'd been asking Brooke to marry him because he wanted her. Not just her body or a quickie against the door but her, Brooke Bonner. Hadn't he said as much?

And what had she done?

The one thing Kyle Morgan had told her not to do because it'd be the regret of her life. She was perilously close to walking away.

What was she *doing*?

"Brooke?"

Brooke startled. Everyone in the room was staring at her, expecting an answer, maybe? "Yes?"

Kari's smile tightened. "When can we schedule an interview and photo shoot with you, Flash and that beautiful baby boy?" Clearly, she'd already asked once.

How could Brooke schedule interviews and photo shoots? She hadn't spoken to Flash since that awful night! She'd ignored his gifts, his notes.

Brooke looked helplessly at Janet Worthington, her new manager. Janet had heard the whole messy story, mostly so she could successfully run interference in situations like this.

"Who did you have in mind?" Janet asked, keeping her tone cool.

"*People* is our first choice, but we've had offers…" Kari launched into the pros and cons of the print publications.

Brooke tuned it all out because it was nothing but noise.

Because Flash had sent the most thoughtful, charming, *perfect* gifts, starting with a box of jasmine green tea and local clover honey with a note that read, "I will never stop fighting for you and Bean."

The next day, a sampler of black teas and a different honey—wildflower—had been delivered. "I have faith in you," the note had said.

Every day since, different flavors of tea and honey and occasionally delicate teacups or thermal mugs and, once, even a plastic toy tea set for Bean had shown up, each with a short note written in Flash's scrawl. He missed her. He hoped Bean was letting her sleep and having fun getting out and about. He asked about how the plans for her album were going. Was she doing okay with Kyle and her mother? Did she need anything from him? He'd be there for her.

The last note—the one from yesterday—had said, "I choose you. I want to do the work. You're worth it."

Flash loved her.

He hadn't said the words—it was true—but his love was in every cup of tea she drank, in every bit of honey sweetness.

He wasn't backing her into a corner and he wasn't forcing her to make a choice. Instead, he'd spent the last two weeks showing her how much he cared, and she hadn't responded. Not even to check on him.

Bean fussed. Brooke took the chance to escape. "Is there anything else you need me for?"

Janet got the hint immediately. "We'll get back to you on dates."

Brooke slipped out while Janet settled the details. For two danged weeks, Brooke had been hemming and hawing, asking herself how she could trust him when, really, she'd been trying to figure out how she could trust herself.

She couldn't do it. She couldn't walk away.

All she needed to do was make a leap of faith.

She texted Flash, Where are you?

My hotel room, was the immediate reply. In Nashville.

Relief coursed through her. Still here?

Never left, babe. I might walk away from you and you might walk away from me when we need to calm down, but I will always come back for you. Been hoping you'll come back to me, too.

Dear God, he really did love her. I need to talk to you.

Where?

She was more than half tempted to ask for his room number, but she had a drowsy infant in the back seat. Meet me at my house in half an hour.

Just as she pulled out of the parking lot, Flash texted back, Thank God.

Flash hadn't waited half an hour. He was on Brooke's doorstep less than fifteen minutes later, waiting. Dad hadn't been happy about Flash driving himself, but a man had to do what a man had to do.

Finally.

It'd taken two weeks of every kind of tea and tea accessory known to mankind, but she'd reached out to him.

Please let this be good, he prayed.

Of course, she needed to talk to him, which was kind of a problem because right now, Flash wasn't doing a whole lot of talking. And kissing—good, deep kissing, the kind that led to clothing-optional activities—was also off the table. Nibbling was strictly forbidden.

Stupid busted jaw.

It felt like an eternity before Brooke drove up, and Flash was thrilled to see she was alone except for the baby.

He hurried to open Brooke's door but the next thing he knew, she was in his arms and he was struggling to hold back the tears because for two long, awful weeks he'd been afraid he'd lost her, and Brooke Bonner wasn't the kind of woman a man just got over.

"Missed you," he mumbled into her hair as best he could.

"Missed you, too. Let me put the baby down and then we'll talk?"

Reluctantly he let her go. He held the door for her as she pulled a napping James Frasier out of the back seat and then got the front door for her as she carried the baby inside.

They got Bean into the crib without waking him. Flash wrapped his arm around Brooke's shoulders and held her as they stared at their son.

Yep. This was right. This was where he belonged.

Now he just had to convince Brooke of that.

Silently she led him back down to the library where he'd nearly ruined everything. "God, I'm so sorry," she said, basically launching herself at him. "Your face!"

Flash grunted at the impact but, hell, he could play with the pain. The bruises had mostly faded to sickly greens and yellows, except where he'd had more work done on his jaw. But he knew he still looked terrible.

He picked her up and carried her to the couch—with its now-lumpy cushions. Then he pulled out his tablet and began typing.

"Are you okay?"

She read the message and then stared at him. "What's wrong with your mouth?"

"Broken jaw. Wired shut. Won't be able to do much talking or anything for a few more weeks. I'm officially retired from the rodeo. Doctors say I'm done—can't risk any more damage."

She went pale. "Oh, my God! Flash! I'm so sorry!"

"It's okay, babe," he typed. "Everything's okay as long as I'm with you."

Her eyes got all watery again. "It was all real, wasn't it? The proposals and this huge ring and all that tea and honey and…it's all real, isn't it?"

He nodded and touched his forehead to hers. "Love you," he tried to say.

"Don't talk, babe. You…" She sniffed and he wiped the tears off her cheeks. "You said so much in all your notes. I was just too confused to see it."

He kissed her then, *gently*, before he tucked her against his chest so he could type. "I love you. I think I always have, ever since that first night. But I didn't fight for you then. I let you go and I've regretted it ever since. I don't want to let you go again. I'm going to fight for you and for our family every day of my life."

"Oh, Flash," she whispered through her tears. "I'm so, so sorry because I was doing the same thing I did last time. I shut you out because I was scared. I was doing the exact same thing my mom and Kyle did, and I was wrong. I know you were protecting me, but everything got so screwed up in my mind that…"

"You had to walk away for a little bit," he typed quickly, his heart pounding. "Just to calm down. I understand. I had faith you'd fight for me, too." He swallowed, a raspy sound, and then added, "You are, right?"

Because it'd about kill him if she said no. He could let the rodeo go and the world would keep right on spinning.

But life without Brooke…no, he wasn't about to let her go.

Lawrence men fell hard and fast and forever.

That's what this was. *Forever.*

"I understand now," she told him. "I didn't before. But I talked with my…with Kyle, and he told me he didn't fight for me, didn't try to get right with my mom. He only wanted me when I was easy and talented. But that's not life, is it? It's hard work. That's what I want—someone who's willing to fight for me, who'll stick it out when it gets hard and help make things better. And that's you."

"That's you, too," he typed back, his hands shaking.

She shook her head, tears dripping down her face. "Not enough. I need to fight harder. Not just for you, but for myself. For us."

"We'll work on it," he typed back. He couldn't wait until he could talk to her again. It was damn near impossible to whisper sweet nothings into a girl's ear on a tablet. "Together. We're a team. Today, tomorrow, every day." When she gasped, he gritted his teeth and made the one concession he was willing to make. "We don't have to get married, but the offer stands. It'll always stand. I'm not giving up on you or on us. I want this to work. Every day, I'll prove it to you. That's a promise."

She took the tablet from his hands and tossed it aside. "But…what if I want to get married? Is that something you still want?"

Flash groaned. "Yes," he said out loud, although it sounded like a tire deflating. "God, yes."

"How will it work?" she asked, stroking her fingertips over his busted jaw.

He picked up the tablet again. "I'm done with chasing the rodeo. It's time I did the stay-at-home-dad thing. Go with you on tour. Be there for you. For our family."

"Oh, Flash," she whispered, carefully throwing her arms around his neck. "That's what I want. You and me and our family. With less broken bones, though."

"Working on it," he got out, holding her tight.

Then he set her aside and got to one knee next to the couch, taking her hands in his. She still had on his ring, thank God. She'd worn it this whole time.

"Brooke, would you marry me?" Although it didn't come out exactly right.

"For real?" she asked, her eyes shimmering with tears.

"For real," he replied, kissing her hands.

"Yes, Flash. Because I am always coming back for you, too," she sobbed.

Flash surged to his feet and pulled her into a hug. This was home. Brooke was home. "Thank God," he mumbled.

Thank God, he'd never have to get over Brooke Bonner.

* * * * *

COMING SOON!

We really hope you enjoyed reading this book. If you're looking for more romance, be sure to head to the shops when new books are available on

Thursday 4th April

To see which titles are coming soon, please visit
millsandboon.co.uk/nextmonth